Dear Me, I Found You

A Journey Through Brokenness, Identity, and Redemption

By: G. M. Janes

Inspired Forever Books
Dallas, Texas

Dear Me, I Found You
A Journey Through Brokenness, Identity, and Redemption

Inspired Forever Books
Dallas, Texas
(214) 487-2220
https://inspiredforeverbooks.com
"Words with Lasting Impact™"

Library of Congress Control Number: 2025909248

Paperback ISBN 13: 978-1-948903-92-9

Printed in the United States of America

Disclaimer: This book is intended for informational and inspirational purposes only and is not a substitute for professional advice, diagnosis, or treatment.

Readers are encouraged to seek qualified, licensed professionals for any concerns related to mental, emotional, physical, legal, or financial well-being. The insights shared in this book are based on personal experiences and should not be considered professional guidance in those areas.

By reading this book, you acknowledge that you are responsible for your own decisions and actions.

Dedication

To Brittany –

My best friend, my anchor, and the love that steadied me when the storm was loud. Thank you for believing in the man I could be, even when I couldn't see him myself.

To Rileigh, Preston, Noah, and Landon –

You are the reason I keep becoming. Your laughter, your questions, your hugs – they remind me every day that love leaves a legacy. This is part of mine, and it's for you.

Prologue

Why I Wrote This Book

I didn't write this book because I had all the answers. I wrote it because for most of my life, I was drowning in questions.

Questions about who I was.

Why I always felt like I wasn't enough.

Why the wounds I never asked for still shaped
so much of who I became.

Why the world seemed to demand a version of me I didn't know
how to be.

This story is not a polished tale of victory. It's a raw journey through brokenness, identity, pain, healing, and redemption. It's a breadcrumb trail through the wilderness of insecurity, adoption, bullying, failed relationships, depression, and the slow, stumbling walk toward grace.

Each chapter begins with a letter—written to a version of myself I once was or a person who left an imprint on my story. These letters aren't just for me. They're for anyone who has ever wondered if they mattered. If their pain was too much. If their story was too messy to be worth telling.

Why It Matters

Because there are too many people walking around believing the lie that their scars make them less lovable. That if others saw the full picture, they'd run. That they're too broken to be whole again.

If that's you—I wrote this book for you.

You're not alone.

You're not too far gone.

You're not beyond healing.

The chapters in this book won't offer you a quick fix. But they will offer you a mirror—and maybe, just maybe, some language for the ache you've been carrying in silence.

My Goal

My goal isn't to impress you. It's to sit beside you.

To meet you in your pain.

To remind you that even when it feels like everything is falling apart, there's still a thread of hope worth holding on to.

I want this book to be a conversation. A safe place. A gentle invitation to finally stop running from your story and begin reclaiming it—one letter, one chapter, one breath at a time.

We heal through truth.

We heal through grace.

And sometimes, we heal simply by being reminded that we're not alone.

Thanks for opening these pages.

Now let's begin.

—Matt Janes

*"Sometimes the beginning of healing looks
a lot like falling apart."*

—*Unknown*

Table of Contents

Chapter 1:

The Breaking Point

Dear Me (Today),

You're here because you're exhausted—from the pretending, from the weight of carrying everyone else's expectations, from the hollow sound your own voice makes in your head. You've reached the edge of something, and you're scared it might be the end. But I'm here to tell you—this is a beginning.

Write it down. The truth. The ache. The moments you thought you wouldn't survive but did. This isn't for them. It's for you. To remember who you were before the world told you who to be.

These letters are a map. One I hope leads you home.

You're not broken. You're breaking open.

Let's begin.

—Micah

Micah stared at the blank page for an hour. The journal had been a gift from Eliza—dark brown leather, soft as worn hands, the kind that smelled like old books and beginnings. He had tucked it away on a shelf for months, too afraid to touch it. Not because he didn't want to write—but because he wasn't sure if he wanted to remember.

But tonight, something was different. Maybe it was the silence. Maybe it was the way the light from the kitchen filtered in through the doorway, casting long shadows across the floor. Maybe it was just time.

He picked up the pen. Let it hover. And then, slowly, the words came.

Dear Me...

The truth had to start somewhere. For most of his life, Micah had been running—toward approval, away from shame, around the questions that kept him up at night. But now, for the first time, he was ready to stop. To stand still. To trace the lines of his life without turning away.

He wasn't writing a book.

He was writing a reckoning.

A catalog of moments. A breadcrumb trail through the darkness. A collection of truths he was finally brave enough to face.

He wrote until his fingers cramped, until his eyes burned, until the page was no longer blank but full of breath and blood and memory.

And when he finished the first letter, he closed the journal gently, as if tucking in his inner child.

This wasn't healing. Not yet.

But it was the beginning of it.

Chapter 1: The Breaking Point

The beginning of coming home.

The sound of a clock ticking filled the silence. It felt like hours passed while he sat with the journal in front of him, lost in thoughts that spiraled around his mind. He had always been afraid to face the truths he had tucked away—afraid of what would happen if he looked too closely at the scars.

He felt a lump rise in his throat as he considered all the ways he had tried to escape himself—through relationships, work, busyness, even distractions like alcohol. It had worked for a time, enough to keep him from truly seeing who he had become. But now, sitting in the quiet of his own living room, Micah knew that avoiding the pain was no longer an option.

He had come to the point where healing wasn't something he could avoid. He had to face it.

He reached for the pen again. His hand shook slightly, but he wrote again, pushing through the resistance in his chest. He didn't need answers. Not yet. He just needed to write it down, to release the feelings that had been locked inside for so long.

I've been running for years. Running from the things I can't change, from the things that haunt me, from the things that could tear me apart if I let them. I've built a life around the idea of avoiding pain, but the truth is—it's only gotten heavier.

He paused, reading the words. It was hard to admit. Hard to admit that he had spent so much of his life not truly living, just getting by, just surviving. The weight of everything he had been trying to avoid—memories, regrets, mistakes—pressed down on him, and he almost couldn't breathe.

But then, something in him shifted.

But I'm here. Still here.

The truth was a strange comfort. It was ugly, raw, and painful, but it was real. And for the first time in a long time, Micah felt like he was beginning to reconnect with the part of himself he had lost somewhere along the way.

The pen kept moving as he wrote, his thoughts spilling onto the page faster than he could process them.

I've always felt like I'm not enough. Like I'm missing something. I've wanted approval from everyone, but I've never been able to give it to myself. I've sought validation in all the wrong places, hoping someone else's love could fill the void.

The words didn't stop. As if once he had started, there was no turning back. Everything that had been buried beneath the surface for so long began to come out, unbidden, unstoppable. The deeper he dug, the more he uncovered—the hurt, the shame, the fear. And yet, he wrote on.

The first few pages were the hardest, but soon it felt less like a burden and more like something he had to do. A release. A letting go.

Micah finally put the pen down when the pages were full. He closed the journal, his heart racing, his mind spinning, but also oddly calm. For the first time in years, he didn't feel like he was running.

It wasn't a solution. He knew that. But it was the beginning.

The beginning of facing what had been left behind. The beginning of healing. He didn't know where it would take him, but he was ready to find out.

And that was enough for now.

"I will not leave you as orphans; I will come to you."

John 14:18 (NIV)

Chapter 2:

To the Boy Who Was Chosen

Dear Me (Age 4),

They said you were chosen. Special. Loved. And you were. But I know there was still a question buried beneath that truth: Why didn't she keep me?

You never asked it out loud. You were too young to form the words, but old enough to feel the absence.

You smiled for pictures and learned quickly how to be "easy"—because somewhere inside, you believed that being difficult meant being unwanted.

But hear me now: you weren't hard to love. You were just hurt.

And you were never the mistake.

Love,
Me

Micah remembered the way the word "chosen" had been repeated to him over the years like a golden badge pinned to his heart. Adults said it with warm eyes and soft voices, like it was supposed to make everything okay. "You were chosen," they told him. "You were picked out of all the others. That means you're special."

And maybe it did. But it also made him feel... different.

He wasn't raised to feel like an outsider. His parents were good people—gentle, kind, supportive. They tucked him in at night, kissed his forehead, told him they loved him. They celebrated his victories and dried his tears. But still, there was something inside of him—something quieter than a whisper—that wouldn't go away.

A question he didn't know how to ask, not when he was four, not even at ten.

Why didn't she want me?

That question would live in the silence between sentences. It would echo in the moments when no one was watching—when he was alone in his room, staring at the ceiling, listening to the creaks in the walls and the hum of the world outside. It would surface in the ache of birthdays and family gatherings when he couldn't help but wonder who he looked like, or what she might be doing, or if she ever thought about him at all.

He grew up learning how to blend in. He smiled for every photo, tried to be polite, obedient, and careful not to cause trouble. Somewhere along the way, he started to believe that love was earned—that if he performed well enough, stayed quiet enough, stayed easy enough, he could keep the love he'd been given.

Because deep down, he feared that love could be taken away—just like it had been before.

That fear made him into a people-pleaser. He became the kid who always said sorry, even when he didn't know what for. He got good at anticipating what others needed from him and became that person. But in doing so, he buried parts of himself. His emotions, his confusion, his pain—he locked those things away so deep, even he lost sight of them.

He remembered once, sitting beside his mom on the couch, looking at old baby pictures. He turned to her and asked, "Why did you choose me?"

His mother didn't hesitate. She pulled him close, ran her fingers gently through his hair, and said, "We didn't choose you, sweetheart. You were always meant to be ours."

He smiled. He wanted so badly to believe her. Part of him did. But part of him still held onto that tiny, lingering question: *Then why did it feel like I didn't belong?*

As he got older, the question didn't go away. It just changed shape.

In middle school, it looked like insecurity. He'd wonder why he didn't have his mom's smile or his dad's nose. He'd search for pieces of himself in strangers' faces.

In high school, it looked like performance. He joined every club, got good grades, tried to be everything to everyone, hoping someone would finally look at him and say, *you're exactly what we needed.*

But no one ever did—not in a way that filled the void.

It wasn't until adulthood that he finally started to unravel the truth.

The problem was never the adoption. The problem was the lie he believed: that he wasn't enough unless he proved it.

Micah had to learn—through tears, therapy, and the love of people who didn't give up on him—that being chosen didn't mean he was a consolation prize. It didn't mean he was plan B. It meant he was loved intentionally, not by accident.

And it also meant that love had nothing to do with being perfect.

He came to see that his parents' love wasn't transactional. It wasn't something he earned through good behavior or easy days. It was steadfast. It had been there all along—strong enough to hold space for his questions, patient enough to wait for his healing.

Micah began to forgive the four-year-old boy who thought he had to smile all the time to be wanted. He started to embrace the boy who felt lost, and confused, and heartbroken by a decision he never had a say in.

He learned to speak kindness over that boy's life. To tell him that he was *never* hard to love. That his pain was real, and it mattered. And most importantly—that he had always been worthy of love, exactly as he was.

There came a time when he stopped asking if he was chosen and started believing that he was *home*.

Not because he earned it.

Not because he made it easy.

But because he was always meant to be.

"You don't have to attend every battle you're invited to."

—Unknown

Chapter 3:

To the Ones Who Drew the Line

Dear Classmates,

You didn't need to throw punches to leave scars. You didn't need to say it to my face—your silence said enough. The way you looked at me. The way you didn't.

The way you made space for each other but never for me.

You called it teasing. Joking. Just part of growing up. But I learned to fold into myself in rooms where I should have stood tall. I learned that it was safer not to try than to be humiliated for failing. I became the quiet kid. The weird one. The boy who stopped raising his hand even when he knew the answer.

But here's what I know now: I wasn't the problem. I was just different—and different scared you. I forgive you, not because you deserve it, but because I deserve peace.

—Micah

Elementary school was supposed to be soft edges and safety. Laughter and Play-Doh. Storytime and recess. But for Micah, it was none of that. It was tight chests and fake smiles. Eyes scanning rooms for exits and safe corners.

It started with the little things. A glance. A smirk. The way kids moved their desks just slightly away when he sat too close. The whispered words behind cupped hands. Words he couldn't always hear but could always feel.

He learned to read between the lines—the quick inside jokes, the sudden hush when he walked into a room, the forced laugh when someone made him the punchline.

It wasn't every kid. But it was enough.

Enough to make him feel like he didn't belong. Enough to make him dread Monday mornings. Enough to make a little boy start questioning his own worth before he could even spell the word.

By second grade, he already knew how to disappear.

He stopped talking unless someone asked him something directly. Even then, his answers were short, calculated. Safe. He lowered his hand even when he knew the answer. He started faking stomachaches to avoid gym class, where teams were picked, and he was always last.

He pretended not to notice when they snickered as he walked by. He kept his head down when they made fun of the way he ran, the way he dressed, the way he didn't quite fit into their boxes.

They called it teasing.

They said it was harmless.

They said kids are just like that.

But Micah felt it like shrapnel—small pieces that never fully healed.

By third grade, he stopped trying to fit in and started trying not to be seen.

He sat alone at lunch, poking at his food while pretending he didn't care. He spent recess wandering near the fence line, kicking at pebbles while the others played tag and four square. If someone laughed nearby, his chest tightened. If someone talked to him, he waited for the joke.

He found comfort in drawing. His notebooks were filled with superheroes and creatures from far-off worlds. They always had powers. They were always strong. They always saved the day—and they were always alone.

By middle school, the jokes slowed. They weren't said out loud anymore, but the looks remained. The exclusion continued. No one shoved him into lockers, but no one saved him a seat, either.

Teachers praised his manners. His good grades. His calmness.

They didn't see the storm beneath the surface. They didn't see the effort it took just to walk into a classroom. To exist in a space where he always felt like an intruder.

Micah began to think maybe it was his fault. Maybe if he dressed differently. Talked less. Talked more. Tried harder. Tried less.

He constantly questioned what part of himself had triggered their rejection.

Was it the way he looked? The way he talked? The way he held himself?

So he shaped himself into smaller and smaller versions, hoping that if he shrank enough, he'd finally fit.

But no matter how much he adjusted, it never felt like enough.

By high school, he had learned to mimic belonging. He smiled when expected. Nodded during small talk. Even made a few acquaintances—surface-level connections that never reached his heart.

People thought he was quiet by choice. Mysterious. Focused.

The truth? He was exhausted.

Exhausted from years of wondering why he wasn't good enough to be invited in. Tired of guarding himself from every laugh, every look, every possible rejection.

But he still showed up.

Day after day, he walked those hallways, even when it felt like walking through a minefield.

And that... was strength.

He didn't realize it at the time. He thought strength looked like popularity, confidence, a crowd of friends around a lunch table. But later—much later—he saw it for what it was.

Real strength was showing up when everything inside him told him to run.

Real strength was sitting alone and still choosing kindness.

Real strength was the belief, however small, that he mattered.

Years later, when he finally began to unpack the damage, Micah was surprised by how deep the wounds still ran. But he also found something else buried under the rubble:

Resilience.

He hadn't let their rejection become his identity. He hadn't let their silence become his voice.

And the boy who once shrank to make others comfortable?

He started standing up. Not with anger. Not with bitterness. But with grace.

Because he had something they never did—perspective.

He could look back and see that they were just kids, scared of anything different. He could see their laughter for what it was: insecurity dressed as cruelty.

And most importantly, he could let it go.

He didn't need revenge. He didn't need apologies. He needed peace.

And peace came when he realized: He had always been enough. They just didn't see it.

But now?

He does.

*"Man looks at the outward appearance,
but the Lord looks at the heart."*

1 Samuel 16:7 (NIV)

Chapter 4:

To the Mask I Wore Too Well

Dear Me (The Performer),

You got really good at pretending, didn't you?

You smiled when you wanted to scream. You said "I'm fine" when you were falling apart. You learned to read a room faster than you learned to read your own heart.

You thought being strong meant being silent. Being likable meant being agreeable. Being loved meant being whatever they needed you to be.

But that wasn't love. That was survival.

I know you were just trying to stay safe. I know you thought the mask was the only way to belong.

But hear me now: you're allowed to be seen. The real you. The messy you. The one with questions and cracks and feelings too big for your chest.

You don't have to perform to be worthy. You just have to be.

—Micah

Micah didn't put on the mask all at once.

Like most survival tactics, it was built one piece at a time.

The first time he realized he could win someone over with a smile, he kept smiling. The first time staying quiet avoided an argument, he kept his voice tucked away. The first time agreeing made him feel safe, he learned to nod even when he wanted to scream "no."

He didn't think of it as deception—it was adaptation.

At home, conflict felt like walking through a minefield. So he became the peacekeeper. The "easy one." The one who didn't ask for much.

At school, he learned quickly that questions made you a target and standing out was risky. So he mastered blending in.

At church, vulnerability was framed as weakness unless it came wrapped in a testimony already tied with a bow. So Micah learned to share the edited version of himself—the one with just enough struggle to be relatable but not enough to be a problem.

He learned to curate his personality like a playlist—picking and choosing the traits people responded well to, muting the ones that felt too much.

And people loved it.

They praised his maturity. His kindness. His reliability.

But no one saw the internal exhaustion.

Micah was praised for being calm, but he was anxious constantly. He was labeled dependable, but the weight of expectations kept him up at night. People said he was easy to be around—but that was only true because he never let them close enough to challenge it.

He was performing. Constantly.

And deep down, he hated it.

Because no matter how many people liked the version of himself he presented, none of them truly knew him.

He would go home after events and replay conversations, wondering if he'd said too much or too little. Wondering if he was too loud, too quiet, too weird, too boring. He'd scroll through social media comparing himself to people who seemed effortlessly authentic while he felt like a walking highlight reel.

Micah built walls so high even he couldn't see over them.

He thought if he controlled how people saw him, he could control whether they stayed.

But the cost was unbearable.

He began to lose his ability to identify what he actually wanted. He would stare at a menu for ten minutes, unsure if he liked chicken tenders or if he'd just ordered them so many times for the sake of familiarity. He couldn't tell if he liked his hobbies or if he just liked being praised for them.

He'd sit with friends, laughing at jokes that didn't feel funny, making small talk that felt like static. They'd say, "You're always so easygoing," and he'd smile while something inside him begged to be known.

The loneliness wasn't from lack of people—it was from lack of connection.

Then one day, it cracked.

It wasn't a big, dramatic unraveling. It was a subtle, sacred shift.

A friend he trusted asked, "Are you really, okay?"

The answer was ready. He'd rehearsed it a thousand times: "Yeah, I'm good. Just tired. Long week."

But for some reason, that day… the script didn't come.

Instead, a whisper inside—one that had been silenced for years—said, *Tell the truth*.

And Micah did.

"No," he said, voice soft but steady. "I'm not okay."

The room didn't go silent. His friend didn't panic. Nothing shattered.

In fact, something beautiful happened.

His friend didn't look away. Didn't change the subject. Didn't try to fix him.

He just nodded. "Thanks for telling me."

Micah cried that night.

Not because he was sad, but because he was finally seen—and the world didn't fall apart.

That moment didn't solve everything. But it cracked the mask enough to let light in.

From that day forward, Micah began practicing honesty. Not in grand, vulnerable speeches—but in simple confessions. "I don't know." "That hurt." "I'm tired." "I need help."

He started giving himself permission to feel.

He stopped saying yes to things just to avoid guilt. He started letting people in, slowly. Hesitantly. But intentionally.

He learned that boundaries weren't barriers to love—they were bridges to it.

He discovered that the people who truly cared didn't want the polished version of him—they wanted *him*.

The messy. The healing. The searching. The growing.

Micah was finding freedom not in becoming someone new, but in returning to who he was before the world told him to edit himself.

He no longer wanted to be known for being agreeable.

He wanted to be known. Period.

And now?

He's still learning. Still catching himself slipping the mask back on. Still reminding himself that performance is not the price of love.

But more than ever, he's showing up as himself.

One unfiltered conversation at a time.

One honest answer at a time.

One brave, maskless moment at a time.

Because the world doesn't need more polished versions of people.

It needs people who are real.

And Micah?

He's finally learning to be one of them.

"Even the smallest light can shine in the darkest night."

—Unknown

Chapter 5:

To the Almost Normal Years

Dear Me (Middle School),

You were starting to believe it might be okay. The air didn't always feel heavy. The hallways weren't always lined with fear. For a little while, you got to breathe.

It wasn't perfect, but it was almost normal. And that mattered more than you knew.

You started laughing again. You found a few people who didn't expect you to be anyone else. You tasted something that looked like hope.

You were healing, even if you didn't know it. And I'm proud of you for letting yourself try.

—Micah

Junior high is supposed to be strange. Everyone is growing too fast—or not fast enough. Voices crack, lockers slam, and awkward moments become currency. But for Micah, those years came with something unexpected: *relief.*

After the emotional landmine that was elementary school, where rejection waited around every corner, middle school felt almost… calm. Not entirely, and not all at once. But it was the first time in a long time that the world didn't feel like it was actively trying to break him.

The sharp edges of childhood cruelty had started to dull. The same kids who used to mock him now seemed too distracted by their own social puzzles to keep up the act. Some had even grown quieter themselves, wrapped in the uncertainty of adolescence.

Micah noticed the change, but he didn't trust it at first. The hurt still lingered. He still scanned the cafeteria before choosing a seat. He still braced himself for laughter when he spoke in class. But slowly, day by day, his shoulders began to lower. His eyes stopped darting. He breathed a little easier.

And then, in seventh grade, *Jared* showed up.

Jared was all energy and quirks—lanky limbs, a quick wit, and a collection of comic books always sticking out of his backpack. He had an encyclopedic knowledge of movies from the 80s and a laugh that sounded like it had been set free after years of captivity. What set Jared apart, though, was this: he saw Micah, and he didn't treat him like a question mark.

He sat down beside him at lunch one day and started talking like they'd been friends for years. No awkward introduction. No hesitation. Just a simple act of presence—and it made all the difference.

That lunch table became something sacred.

It was never a huge group—just four boys who didn't quite fit anywhere else. Each one had their own brand of oddness, and none of them apologized for it. They quoted lines from old movies. Debated who the best superhero was. Turned the weirdest topics into full-blown lunchtime debates. It was chaotic and loud and messy.

But it was *safe*.

Micah didn't have to perform for them. He didn't have to try to be cool or funny or invisible. He could just exist. And for the first time in a long time, that felt like *enough*.

It wasn't all smooth sailing. The insecurities hadn't disappeared—they had just gotten quieter. Every now and then, a voice in his head would whisper that this wouldn't last. That one day the joke would be on him again. But those whispers didn't control him anymore.

Micah started trying things.

He joined the drama club, where he discovered the thrill of stepping into someone else's story. He enrolled in art class and lost himself in colors and shapes. He even agreed to sing a short solo during a choir performance—his hands shaking behind the curtain, his heart pounding in his ears—but he did it anyway.

Afterward, a teacher pulled him aside and said, "You're coming out of your shell."

Micah smiled, but part of him wanted to say, *It's not a shell. It was armor. And I'm finally learning how to take it off.*

The fear wasn't gone. But now, it didn't win.

He still had days when he came home and shut his door just to be alone. Still had nights when old wounds itched under the surface. Still caught himself holding his breath when someone laughed too hard nearby.

But there was also light now. Laughter that was shared instead of feared. Conversations that weren't loaded with barbs. Places where he felt like he *belonged*.

Micah started writing in secret. Not homework or essays—but *stories*. His own little universes where the quiet kid was always the hero. Where the overlooked one saved the world. Where bravery looked like kindness, and victory looked like standing back up.

Those stories became therapy before he ever knew what therapy was.

He didn't write for recognition. He wrote to survive. To process. To believe that maybe his voice mattered—even if only to him.

Middle school wasn't magical. It was still awkward and loud and confusing. But it gave Micah something he hadn't had before:

Permission to hope.

Hope that things could get better. That friends could be real. That maybe, just maybe, who he was… was enough.

Healing didn't arrive with fanfare. It didn't come with an announcement or a certificate. It came quietly—in the smile of a friend, in the safety of a lunch table, in the courage to try something new.

It came in *almost normal*.

And that was a miracle.

Because once you taste almost normal, you start to believe in *something more*.

And that belief?

It was the beginning of everything.

*"A friend loves at all times, and a brother
is born for a time of adversity"*

Proverbs 17:17 (NIV)

Chapter 6:

To the Friends Who Stayed

Dear You (The Ones Who Stayed),

You didn't ask for the highlight reel. You didn't flinch at the messy stuff. You didn't demand explanations. You didn't ask me to change. You just stayed.

You sat beside me when I didn't know how to speak. You showed up when I wasn't sure I wanted company. You laughed when I forgot how. You reminded me what it felt like to belong.

You weren't loud. You weren't perfect.

But you were there.

And that saved me in ways I still don't have the words for.

—Micah

Micah didn't trust easily. Not because he didn't want to. But because trusting had cost him too much in the past.

People had smiled to his face and disappeared when things got complicated. They praised his strength but vanished when he was weak. Love often came with conditions—spoken or implied: Be agreeable. Be inspiring. Be strong. Be less. Be easy to handle, and maybe… just maybe, you'll be worth keeping.

So he learned to stay guarded.

He had friends—sure. Acquaintances, coworkers, surface-level companions who were good for a laugh or a quick check-in. People who came to parties and signed group cards and asked how he was doing without expecting a real answer.

But very few knew the real Micah.

The one who overanalyzed every word he said after a conversation. The one who sometimes shut down for days at a time. The one who wrestled with dark thoughts and heavy feelings and didn't always know how to reach out for help.

He had learned to keep people just close enough to feel connected—but never close enough to become a burden.

Then came the ones who stayed.

He didn't know what made them different at first. Maybe it was timing. Maybe it was grace. Maybe it was just the quiet, sacred courage of people who know how to love without needing applause.

They weren't flashy. They weren't loud. They didn't barge into his life waving red flags of rescue.

They just kept showing up.

There was the friend who, sensing something was off, dropped off coffee with a sticky note that read, "You don't have to talk. Just wanted to remind you that you matter."

There was the one who sent a dumb meme at midnight because he knew Micah probably wasn't sleeping. The one who texted, "You don't have to respond, but I'm not going anywhere." The one who invited him to sit in silence—not to fix him, but to sit with him in it.

Micah remembered one night in particular.

He had hit a wall—emotionally, mentally, spiritually. It was one of those weeks where getting out of bed felt like a marathon. He canceled plans, ignored texts, and let dishes pile up in the sink like some silent reflection of everything he didn't have the energy to deal with.

He didn't expect anyone to notice.

But then… a knock at the door.

He almost didn't answer. But curiosity beat out shame.

It was a friend holding a pizza box and a six-pack, shrugging like it was the most casual thing in the world. "Didn't feel like eating alone. Mind if I crash here?"

They didn't talk about the heaviness that night. They just sat on the couch, eating cold pizza and watching reruns of a show neither of them really liked. But the silence felt safe. Sacred, even.

Micah didn't have to be "on." Didn't have to smile. Didn't have to explain.

And that night, something inside him began to soften.

These friends—this quiet, faithful handful of humans—taught him that presence doesn't always look like grand gestures. Sometimes, it looks like being the person who stays when things get awkward. Or quiet. Or unbearably heavy.

They didn't pressure him to heal faster. They didn't demand he be okay. They just made space.

They didn't need perfection. They just needed permission. Permission to sit beside the sadness. To celebrate the small wins. To check in without needing something in return.

And slowly, Micah let himself believe something he'd never truly accepted:

That maybe—just maybe—he was worth loving even when he didn't have anything to offer.

He remembered a moment when one of them said, "You don't scare me."

That line undid him.

Because Micah had always feared that the real him—the anxious, unsure, weary version—would be too much. That if anyone saw it clearly, they'd run.

But these friends stayed.

They stayed when the texts were short and distant. They stayed when the smile was forced. They stayed when the light left his eyes for a while.

And Micah began to believe that real friendship wasn't about being easy to love. It was about being worth the effort.

Healing didn't come in some grand, sweeping moment. It came in pieces—tender, unglamorous, often unexpected.

In a shared playlist.

A whispered prayer.

A laugh over something stupid that reminded him what joy felt like.

These friends didn't fix his life. But they gave him room to breathe.

Room to stop pretending.

Room to be seen.

Room to be *real*.

And that changed everything.

Now, years later, Micah doesn't have hundreds of close friends. But the ones he has? They've seen him—truly seen him.

And still… they stayed.

He's learning that friendship doesn't have to mean constant contact. It means consistent care. It means showing up in the ways you can, when you can.

The ones who stayed taught him that sometimes love doesn't roar—it whispers. And sometimes, the whisper is enough to keep someone here.

Now, Micah tries to be that kind of friend too.

The kind who doesn't flinch at the mess.

The kind who isn't scared of silence.

The kind who stays—not because it's easy, but because it's *worth it*.

Because the world is full of people wearing masks, barely holding on.

And sometimes, all it takes is one person willing to sit beside them, pizza box in hand, saying,

"I'm not going anywhere."

Micah carries those moments now—etched into the fabric of his story.

Not just the laughs. Not just the light. But the sacred, healing stillness of friends who stayed in the dark…

until he remembered how to find the light again.

"Sometimes people come into your life just to show you that you deserve to be noticed."

—Unknown

Chapter 7:

To the Girl Who Made Me Feel Seen

Dear Her,

You were the first person who looked at me and didn't flinch.

You saw me—really saw me—and something about that made me feel whole, if only for a little while.

I didn't know what love was. I just knew that when you smiled, the noise inside me quieted.

I thought maybe you were the cure for everything I didn't understand about myself.

I should've told you the truth. About the pain. About the fear.

But I was too afraid that once you saw behind the mask, you'd leave. So I kept wearing it.

You weren't my redemption, and you never should've had to be.

But thank you—for making me feel worthy of being seen. Even if just for a little while.

Love,
Micah

She came into Micah's life like a whisper in a room full of noise.

He didn't know he was waiting for her. He didn't know how much he needed someone to simply *notice* him—not for what he could do, not for how he fit in, but just… as he was.

Her name was Hannah.

And in a world where Micah had learned to shrink, to stay quiet, to avoid taking up space, Hannah walked in like she had always belonged. She didn't try to fix him. She didn't press him with questions he wasn't ready to answer. She just offered her presence like a gift—and for the first time, someone's presence felt safe.

Hannah was light. Not the blinding, overwhelming kind. She was the soft kind—the kind that made the shadows in his life a little less dark. She had a laugh that sounded like it belonged in a world without pain, and when she laughed with *him*, it made him believe he might not be broken after all.

Micah didn't fall in love all at once. It happened slowly, in the quiet spaces.

In the way she saved him a seat without asking. In the way she remembered the things he said in passing and brought them up days later, proving she was actually *listening*. In the way she didn't fill the silence with pity, but just let it be—comfortable, calm.

With her, he started to feel human again.

Not the shell he had become. Not the version of himself he projected to survive. But *himself*—awkward, quiet, complicated, and maybe even a little funny.

They shared hours of conversations—some deep, some meaningless, all comforting. They walked hallways side by side, laughed over stupid inside jokes, passed notes during class like something out of a movie.

And slowly, Micah let himself believe.

He believed he could be wanted without having to perform. That he could matter to someone without bending to fit their expectations. That maybe—just maybe—he was worth loving.

But even then, he kept the mask on.

Not because he wanted to deceive her—but because he didn't trust that anyone could love what was *underneath*.

Micah had spent years perfecting the art of pretending. Pretending he wasn't hurt. Pretending he wasn't scared. Pretending he didn't still carry the echoes of a lonely childhood in his chest.

So when Hannah looked at him with kindness, he smiled. He nodded. He gave her the parts of himself he thought were acceptable, palatable. He held back the rest.

He never told her about the panic that sometimes gripped him for no reason. Or the way he still felt like a ghost in rooms filled with people. Or the shame he carried from years of being "too much" or "not enough."

He thought she might run if she saw the full picture. He couldn't bear to lose the one person who made him feel seen.

So he wore the mask—and hoped it would be enough.

But the thing about masks is they create distance. Not intentionally, not cruelly—but inevitably.

And one day, without a dramatic ending or bitter words, she was gone.

They drifted, as young people often do. Life moved forward. Conversations grew shorter. The magic faded. And just like that, the girl who had once made him feel so visible became part of the past.

Micah didn't cry. Not in front of anyone. But he felt the loss in his bones.

He spent weeks wondering what he did wrong. Was it something he said? Or didn't say? Was he not enough? Or too much? He replayed memories like scenes from a movie, looking for clues.

But deep down, he knew. He had never truly let her in. Not all the way.

He wanted to be loved, but he hadn't believed he could be— not if someone saw *everything*.

It wasn't until much later—years down the road—that Micah understood what she had really given him.

It wasn't love in the way the world defined it. It wasn't perfect. It wasn't lifelong.

But it was real.

She had seen *him*. The real him. Even if only in glimpses. Even if he didn't let her all the way in. She had chosen to sit next to him, to talk to him, to laugh with him—without asking for anything in return.

And that mattered.

She hadn't saved him. But she had *touched* something inside him. Something he didn't even know was still alive.

Hope.

The hope that he could be known and still accepted.

Micah would carry that with him long after she was gone. Not as a regret—but as a reminder.

That love—real love—doesn't always come to stay. But sometimes it comes to *show us who we are*. And who we *could* be.

And for that, he would always be grateful.

"Be still, and know that I am God."

Psalm 46:10 (NIV)

Chapter 8:

To the Boy Who Couldn't Stop Running

Dear Me (The Runner),

You spent your life running.

Running from pain. From questions. From silence.

You thought that if you ran far enough, fast enough, it wouldn't catch up with you.

But the truth is, it always does. It was never the distance that mattered—it was the stopping.

And you're still learning to stop. To stand still. To let yourself be seen.

And that's brave.

You don't have to outrun it. You just have to let it catch you—and then choose to heal.

—Micah

Micah didn't always realize he was running.

At first, it just looked like staying busy. Saying yes to everything. Throwing himself into school, into sports, into anything that kept him moving fast enough to not feel the slow ache under the surface. He didn't recognize it for what it was—not until years later, when the running turned into restlessness, and restlessness into exhaustion.

He had always been the kid who needed a reason to stay distracted. Who feared silence more than confrontation. Who would rather be overwhelmed than alone with his thoughts. Because when everything stopped, the voices came—the memories, the doubts, the unanswered questions about where he belonged, about who he really was.

So he ran.

At first emotionally. Then physically. Then with everything he had. The military seemed like a perfect hiding place.

Structure. Discipline. Constant motion. Camaraderie without intimacy. Purpose without vulnerability. It offered just enough belonging to soothe the ache, and just enough distraction to keep the questions at bay.

In uniform, Micah found a kind of armor. Not just the one issued to him, but one built from years of rehearsed strength and quiet desperation. No one asked about his childhood wounds or emotional scars. They just asked if he could show up, follow orders, carry weight.

He could do that. He could carry weight. He'd been doing it long before the uniform.

But even on deployment—surrounded by dust, duty, and men who masked their own pain with jokes and bravado—Micah couldn't outrun the truth. The truth always found its way back in the quietest hours. In the stillness after a mission. In the eerie silence of a night shift when everyone else was asleep and there was nothing left to distract him.

That was when the questions would whisper again:

Who are you, really? Why do you still feel like you're not enough?

He would clench his fists. Swallow hard. Bury it deeper.

And run faster.

After the military, the running didn't stop. It just changed shape.

He ran into work, into relationships, into responsibilities. Into roles he didn't quite feel equipped to carry. Husband. Father. Provider. Leader. On the outside, he looked put together. On the inside, he was gasping for breath.

He chased approval. Validation. Something that would finally quiet the nagging voice inside that said he was still that scared, unwanted boy trying to prove he mattered.

And when that didn't work, he ran toward the numbing things. Late nights. Isolation. Distractions disguised as productivity. He ran from vulnerability because it made him feel exposed. Weak. Powerless.

But eventually—inevitably—he hit a wall.

It wasn't a single moment. It was a slow unraveling. Missed connections with people he loved. Emotional distance that crept in like a fog. A sense that no matter how hard he tried, he was always one step away from being *found out*.

The mask was cracking. The armor was too heavy. The running was taking more than it gave.

And for the first time in his life, Micah stopped.

It wasn't dramatic. There was no thunderclap, no grand declaration.

Just a quiet moment on a quiet day when he looked in the mirror and didn't recognize himself. And something inside whispered:

You can't keep doing this.

So he stood still. And it terrified him.

Because standing still meant facing everything he'd buried—grief, shame, anger, fear. It meant acknowledging the things he had spent a lifetime trying to escape. It meant allowing the pain to surface and trusting that it wouldn't destroy him.

But he did it anyway. Little by little, he let the pain catch up to him.

He opened up—to a friend, to a counselor, to God. He spoke things he'd never said aloud. He sat in the discomfort of honesty. He learned that healing didn't come from running faster—it came from standing still long enough to *feel*.

And what he found in that stillness was something he hadn't expected:

Compassion.

For himself.

He stopped seeing himself as broken beyond repair and started seeing himself as brave. Brave for surviving. Brave for still hoping. Brave for choosing to face the very things he had spent so long avoiding.

Healing wasn't instant. It wasn't linear. Some days still felt like backslides. Some nights, the old instinct to run returned.

But Micah no longer believed the lie that running would save him.

Now, he knew the truth.

The things we run from don't disappear. They wait. Patiently. Silently. And if we're brave enough to turn around and face them, they stop being monsters in the dark—and start becoming stories we can reclaim.

Micah was still learning to stop. Still learning to let himself be seen. Still learning that he didn't have to carry it all alone.

But every time he chose stillness over escape, every time he chose truth over pretending, he took a step toward the version of himself he was always meant to be.

And that version?

He didn't run.

He *stood*.

Not perfectly. Not fearlessly.

But honestly.

"Courage doesn't always roar. Sometimes courage is the quiet voice at the end of the day saying, 'I will try again tomorrow"

—Mary Anne Radmacher

Chapter 9:

To the Man Who Wore the Uniform

Dear Me (The Soldier),

You wore a uniform. You wore it because you thought it would make you strong.

You thought it would make you someone else—someone worthy.

But what you didn't know is that strength comes from within, not from what you wear.

And worth? That's not something you earn. It's something you already had.

And I'm proud of you for serving.

But I'm even prouder of you for learning to serve yourself—for showing up to the hard places not with armor, but with honesty.

—Micah

Micah didn't join the military just to serve his country.

He joined because he was tired of being no one.

Tired of drifting, tired of questions with no answers, tired of carrying the weight of invisible wounds with nowhere to put them. He thought maybe if he wore the right thing—stood tall, fell in line, followed orders—then the chaos inside him might finally quiet down.

He thought the uniform would give him identity. Respect. Purpose. Maybe even belonging.

And at first, it did.

The structure brought comfort. The discipline brought clarity. The constant motion kept the silence at bay. There were rules to follow, a rank to earn, a mission to complete. It gave him something his past never had—*predictability*.

He was no longer the boy on the outside looking in. He was *in*.

He had a title. A rank. A place to be. And that place felt good.

But beneath the pride and the patches, the boy inside the uniform hadn't really changed.

He still carried the same doubts. The same ache. The same need to prove himself. He thought the salutes and ceremonies would erase the parts of him that still didn't feel like enough.

But when the world got quiet—during long deployments, late-night shifts, and the slow hours between missions—Micah would lie awake and feel it rising again.

The mask hadn't come off. It had just gotten camouflaged.

The same questions still echoed in his mind:

What if they saw the real me? What if I'm not actually strong? What happens when the uniform comes off?

There were moments in combat that tested his body—but it was the moments in stillness that tested his soul.

When the mission was done and the adrenaline wore off, he was left with himself. No orders. No rank. Just the weight of everything he hadn't faced.

He began to see that bravery on the battlefield was only part of the story. The harder battle was the one waiting inside.

Coming home was even more disorienting.

People said thank you. Strangers shook his hand. But few knew how to talk to him about what came next.

And Micah didn't know how to explain it.

He missed the clarity of service—but not the emotional distance it had allowed him to keep.

He missed the brotherhood—but not the fear of being vulnerable.

He missed the mission—but not the silence that came after.

Civilian life didn't come with a playbook. There were no briefings for how to rebuild your identity when you've spent years tying it to a uniform.

Micah wrestled with questions that didn't have simple answers:

Who was he without the structure?

Who was he without the title?

Could he be strong without the role?

For a while, he kept pretending. Showing up. Smiling. Telling people he was fine.

But deep down, the truth was breaking through.

He had joined the military to escape the pain of being unseen. But now, the pain wasn't just behind him—it was *within* him.

And so began a different kind of service.

This time, not to a country. But to himself.

He started going to therapy—not because someone told him to, but because he wanted to stop running. He began reading books about trauma, identity, and healing. He had long, painful conversations with people he trusted. He allowed himself, for the first time, to *feel* everything he had buried.

And slowly, he learned that the real strength wasn't in how many battles he had fought—but in how many truths he was willing to face.

He stopped equating silence with weakness.

He stopped trying to earn worth through performance.

He started to believe that maybe he had been worthy all along.

Micah no longer needed the uniform to feel valid. He no longer needed to perform for approval. His strength now looked different—it looked like vulnerability. It looked like asking for help. It looked like showing up, even when he was afraid.

It looked like a man who had been torn down and decided to rebuild.

Stronger. Wiser. And *seen*.

The boy who once thought being a soldier would make him whole had finally realized something the uniform couldn't teach him:

You can't armor your way to healing.

Real healing only happens when you lay it down—when you let the walls fall, when you allow the wounds to be touched, not hidden.

And that takes more courage than any battlefield ever required.

Micah didn't regret his service. It was part of his story—an honorable chapter that shaped him in many ways.

But what he was most proud of?

Was learning to *serve himself* with the same commitment he once gave to the mission.

Because healing—real healing—is a mission, too. And he was finally ready to complete it.

*"Unless the Lord builds the house,
the builders labor in vain."*

Psalm 127:1 (NIV)

Chapter 10:

To the Marriage Built on Sand

Dear Me (The Husband),

You didn't know how to love her. Not the way she needed, at least.

You wore your own pain like armor, and you couldn't take it off long enough to see her clearly.

You wanted to fix things. But you didn't know how to fix yourself first.

That was never her fault. And it was never your fault either.

But it was your responsibility to face the truth—and you didn't.

I'm sorry. And I forgive you.

—Micah

Micah had always believed that marriage would be the answer.

The finish line. The reward. The place where all the broken pieces would finally come together. For so long, he had dreamed of standing at the altar—vows exchanged, hands held, promises made—and walking into a new life where love could heal everything.

And when that day came, he meant every word he said.

He loved her. Deeply. Fiercely. But somewhere, beneath the tuxedo and the vows and the honeymoon photos, there was a gnawing fear: *What if I'm still not enough?*

He had stepped into marriage hoping it would settle that question. That love would complete what was missing. That intimacy would silence the inner critic that had haunted him since childhood.

But marriage isn't a healing machine. It doesn't mend old wounds by default. If anything, it exposes them.

At first, things felt beautiful. The excitement of building a life together, of sharing inside jokes, of navigating bills and dinners and bedtime routines. There was comfort in the routine, joy in the newness.

But Micah still carried old wounds he hadn't named out loud. Insecurities. Fears. The lingering belief that if he showed too much of himself—his sadness, his failures, his doubts—he'd be left behind again.

And so, without realizing it, he began to hide.

Not in obvious ways. Not with lies or distance. But emotionally. He filtered what he said, buried what he felt, and kept the heaviest parts of himself out of reach. He wanted to protect her from his darkness, but in doing so, he kept her from truly knowing him.

The cracks began small.

Missed signals. Misunderstood words. Arguments that didn't seem to make sense but left both of them hurting. She would ask what was wrong, and he'd say "nothing," because how could he explain something he didn't even fully understand?

She wasn't the enemy. She was kind, patient, and loving. But she needed more than he knew how to give. She needed presence. Openness. Vulnerability. And Micah was still learning how to give those things to *himself*, let alone to someone else.

The tension in their home became a quiet hum—never explosive, but always there.

Micah wanted to fix it. He read books. He apologized. He tried to be better. But nothing stuck, because it was all external. He was trying to rebuild the roof when the foundation had never been poured.

The truth was, he had built their marriage on sand.

Not intentionally. Not carelessly. But still—on sand.

He thought that being a "good husband" meant performing. Providing. Saying the right things and doing the right chores. He didn't realize that true connection required more than performance—it required presence.

And presence meant vulnerability.

It meant showing up even when he was messy.

It meant speaking honestly even when he wasn't sure how it would be received.

It meant letting her see the full picture—not just the parts he had curated.

But he wasn't ready. And the truth is, neither was she.

They were both good people. Both trying. But both still learning how to love themselves—let alone each other.

Eventually, the weight of miscommunication, unmet expectations, and unspoken pain brought everything crashing down. There was no singular betrayal, no dramatic ending. Just a slow, quiet drift apart. A mutual unraveling.

And when it ended, Micah was left with silence.

He could've blamed her. He could've pointed fingers. But somewhere deep down, he knew the truth:

He hadn't shown up as his whole self.

Not because he didn't care—but because he didn't know how.

And yet… he chose not to hate that version of himself.

He chose *compassion*.

Because that version of Micah—the one who wore the ring, said the vows, and tried so hard to be "enough"—was still healing. Still growing. Still learning what love really looked like when it wasn't wrapped in fear.

So he let himself grieve. Not just the marriage, but the illusion that love alone could save him.

And then he did something even harder.

He forgave himself.

He stopped seeing the end of that relationship as a failure and started seeing it as a classroom. One where he learned what real love demands—truth, vulnerability, wholeness.

Micah now knew that the best thing he could offer someone wasn't a polished version of himself—it was *his honest self*.

Because love built on performance crumbles. But love built on truth? That can weather anything.

He didn't hate his ex-wife. He didn't even hate the past. They had both given what they had. They had both tried.

And sometimes, *that* is love, too.

But now, Micah understood that love begins within. Before you can share it, you must learn to offer it inward.

To the boy who was hurting. To the man who didn't know better.

To the version of yourself who kept showing up—even when he was afraid.

That version of Micah wasn't perfect. But he was brave. And now, he was building on something stronger than sand.

And this time, he wasn't building alone.

*"You can't pour from an empty cup.
Take care of yourself first."*

—Unknown

Chapter 11:

To the Love I Tried to Fix Myself

Dear Me (The Fool),

You believed in the lie. The one that said love could fix everything.

You thought if you loved enough, everything would work out.

But love doesn't work that way. Love isn't the cure for all wounds. Love is supposed to be a partnership.

It's supposed to be something you build together—not something you use to cover up the cracks.

I'm sorry for all the lies you told.

But I'm proud of you for finally seeing the truth.

—Micah

Micah had always been a romantic at heart.

Not the kind who memorized movie lines or brought flowers every Friday—but the kind who believed, deeply and stubbornly, that love could save him.

From as early as he could remember, love felt like the promised land. The thing that would finally bring peace to the chaos inside. If he could just find the one, then surely the doubt would fade, the shame would quiet, and the brokenness would finally be made whole.

So he searched for it. Craved it. Gave himself to it far too quickly, too completely. Because he wasn't just looking for love— he was looking for *healing*.

And that was the lie.

The lie that love could patch holes it didn't make.

That another person's affection could rewrite years of insecurity, fear, and rejection.

That if he just gave enough of himself—loved hard enough, sacrificed deep enough—then everything else would fall into place.

Micah didn't see it at first.

Not when he said "I love you" just weeks in.

Not when he bent his boundaries to make things work.

Not when he ignored the voice inside that said, *something about this isn't right.*

He was blinded by the dream. The hope that this time, finally, he had found the answer.

But love—real love—doesn't thrive on desperation. It doesn't grow in the soil of self-denial.

It demands truth. It demands presence. It demands two whole people willing to meet each other in the middle.

Micah wasn't whole. And he wasn't being honest. Not with them, and not with himself.

He wore a mask, one he didn't even realize he had put on. The mask of the perfect partner. The attentive boyfriend. The one who never needed too much, never asked too many questions, never let his wounds show.

Because he believed that if he just played the part well enough, love would eventually earn him healing.

Instead, it earned him heartache.

He clung too tightly. Gave too much too fast. Lost himself in the process.

And when it all started falling apart—when the relationship turned tense, distant, and confusing—he tried harder.

More affection. More attention. More apologies.

He poured himself out, hoping it would be enough to fix what had been broken long before the relationship began.

But love, when used as a cover, eventually collapses under the pressure.

Micah had used it like a patch on a leaking pipe—thinking if he just held it tight enough, he could keep it from bursting.

But it burst. And the aftermath was messy.

There were words he wished he could take back. Wounds he never meant to cause. Nights spent wondering how he could've gotten it so wrong. Days when the loneliness returned louder than ever—because this time, it brought shame with it.

But something happened in that pain.

He finally stopped blaming love for failing him—and started asking why he'd expected it to save him in the first place.

He started facing hard truths. He looked at the patterns. He listened to the voice he had spent years ignoring—the one that said: *you can't pour from an empty cup.*

Micah realized that love wasn't meant to fix him. It was meant to *join* him.

And before anyone could join him on the road ahead, he had to stop walking with a limp he refused to name.

So he began again. Slowly. Quietly.

He stopped rushing. He stopped chasing validation. He started asking better questions—not "Do they love me?" but "Do I love *me?*"

And slowly, the answers changed.

He learned that love wasn't about filling a void. It wasn't about someone else completing him. It was about showing up as himself—*fully, honestly, imperfectly*—and building something real from there.

Micah still believed in love. But not the kind that rescues. The kind that *partners.*

The kind that says, "I see you—not because you've earned it, but because you're here."

He looked back on those old relationships not with bitterness, but with clarity.

They were not failures. They were teachers. They showed him the truth:

That love is not a fix—it's a *choice.*

A choice to walk together. To grow together. To speak truth when it's easier to stay silent.

To stay rooted when things get hard—not because you need each other, but because you *choose* each other.

And before Micah could ever truly choose someone else, he had to finally choose himself.

That was the hardest love of all.

But the most necessary.

"Love bears all things, believes all things, hopes all things, endures all things."

1 Corinthians 13:7 (NIV)

Chapter 12:

To the Girl Who Stayed When It Was Hard

Dear Her (The One Who Stayed),

You didn't fix me. You didn't try to. You just stayed.

And in a world that taught me people don't do that— you did.

You didn't run when I was quiet. Or when I was too loud. Or when I couldn't explain what was wrong.

You stayed.

That's what I remember most.

Not a grand rescue. Just the steady presence of someone who didn't flinch at the mess.

I'm still figuring things out. Still healing. Still learning what love really looks like.

But I'll always be grateful that in one of the darkest chapters—you were there.

—Micah

She didn't come into his life like a storm. She arrived like a pause.

And Micah wasn't sure what to do with that.

Most people had rushed in, filled the silence with noise, offered solutions like prescriptions. Most people hadn't stayed long. They came with intensity, urgency, opinions—and then disappeared just as fast when the weight got too heavy, or the cracks showed too clearly.

But she didn't.

She didn't try to "handle" him. She didn't try to carry his pain like it was her job to lighten it. She simply showed up, over and over, without making it about herself.

And at first, Micah didn't trust it.

He'd been conditioned to expect something different. People either tried to fix him or flee from him. He'd learned to shape-shift in response—become what the room needed, say the right things, hide the parts that weren't palatable.

But she didn't ask for a version of him. She accepted the whole, unpolished, tangled-up version. The one he barely knew how to be around himself.

There were no breakthrough conversations that changed everything. No poetic moment of realization. Just slow, ordinary presence. She remembered small things: how he liked his coffee, the books he'd reread a hundred times, the way he got quiet when he was anxious. She didn't try to pull him out of his silence. She just sat there with him until the silence wasn't so loud.

She didn't say, "You're not broken."

She said, "You're still loved, even if you are."

That hit differently.

It wasn't sugar-coated. It wasn't dismissive. It was real. And real had been hard to come by.

Micah had spent so long feeling like a burden. Like loving him came with fine print, disclaimers, damage reports. But she looked at him like he was whole enough to belong. Not because he had earned it. Not because he had healed. Just because he was.

He still kept his distance at times. Still had walls built out of old betrayals and childhood scars. He wasn't easy to reach. But she never seemed to mind the slow pace. Never pressured him to hurry up and heal so he could be more convenient to love.

She didn't treat him like a project.

She treated him like a person.

And in a life where he'd often felt like a problem to be solved— that was everything.

He started noticing the shift before he could admit it to himself. He laughed more—not the forced kind, but the kind that caught him off guard. He started answering calls again. Started speaking more gently to himself when he messed up. He started believing, just a little, that maybe he didn't have to perform his worth. Maybe it was okay just to be.

Not because she told him so. But because she lived it in the way she treated him.

And it was hard, too. There were moments when his old patterns tried to sabotage it. When his brain said, *push her away before she gets tired of you.* When he'd retreat into silence and expect her to leave like others had.

But she didn't.

She never promised she wouldn't. She didn't make vows or offer guarantees. But her consistency spoke louder than anything she could've said.

Micah didn't fall in love with her because she healed him. He fell in love with her because she didn't ask him to hide while he was healing.

She saw the dark and didn't flinch. She saw the grief that hadn't fully settled and made room for it. She didn't turn it into a sermon. She didn't label him with pity. She didn't make it about herself.

She just loved him quietly, steadily.

Micah had always thought love would come with fireworks. But this... this was like a steady fire in the corner of a cold room. It didn't demand his attention. It just kept burning, reminding him he wasn't alone.

He didn't change overnight. This wasn't a transformation story.

He still had days where the sadness weighed too much. Still had nights where the thoughts raced, and the doubts screamed louder than truth. But she didn't leave when he didn't have a good day. She didn't try to drag him forward. She walked beside him at whatever pace he could manage.

That's what made the difference. She didn't try to rewrite his story. She just refused to walk away from it.

Micah used to think being "saved" meant someone pulling you out of the deep end—heroic, dramatic, drenched in adrenaline. But he was learning something different now.

Sometimes being saved looks like someone treading water next to you. Not trying to carry you. Just staying close enough so you don't forget how to swim.

She wasn't his rescuer.

Chapter 12: To the Girl Who Stayed When It Was Hard

She was his reminder. That love didn't have to hurt. That he didn't have to earn his worth.

That maybe, just maybe—he was allowed to stay.

"Then you will know the truth, and the truth will set you free."

John 8:32 (NIV)

Chapter 13:

To the Lies I Believed Myself

Dear Me (Who Believed the Lies),

You didn't ask to be lied to. But somewhere along the way, you started to believe them.

You believed that if someone left, it must've been your fault. You believed silence meant you weren't worth speaking to.

You believed you had to earn love and prove you belonged. You believed you were too much for some and not enough for others.

You believed that broken meant useless. And you wore those lies like skin. You didn't know they were lies. You just knew they fit.

They shaped your posture.

Your prayers.

Your pace.

They dictated who you thought you were allowed to be. But here's the thing—a lie doesn't become truth just because it's familiar.

And a wound doesn't make you unworthy of healing.

So slowly, painfully, beautifully… you started trading them in.

Lie: You are hard to love.

Truth: You are already loved. Deeply. Just as you are.

Lie: You will always be too much.

Truth: You were never meant to shrink.

Lie: You'll never get it right.

Truth: You were never expected to.

Lie: You're beyond repair.

Truth: You're being made new.

Not all at once. Not cleanly. Not quietly. But steadily. With grace.

You're not who you were. And you're not yet who you'll become.

But thank God, you're no longer who you believed you had to be.

—Micah

Micah remembered the first time he realized he had believed a lie for most of his life.

It wasn't dramatic. No lightning bolt of revelation. Just a quiet moment, sitting in the passenger seat of his own thoughts, letting a friend's words sink in: *"You know that's not true about you, right?"*

He had laughed it off at the time. But the words lingered.

You know that's not true about you, right?

He had spent years becoming a version of himself that could survive. Perform. Impress. Belong. It had worked—on the surface. People liked him. He made others laugh. He showed up, worked hard, stayed strong.

But beneath the surface? He was tired. Not just physically, but soul-deep tired. Tired of always needing to be "okay." Tired of measuring himself by other people's reactions. Tired of wondering if love had to be earned and belonging had an expiration date.

Micah's identity wasn't built on truth. It was built on compensation.

For the father who didn't show up, he compensated by becoming indispensable.

For the rejection he felt in school, he compensated by becoming impressive.

For the ache of never feeling enough, he compensated by trying to be everything to everyone.

And the thing about compensating is—it works.

Until it doesn't.

Eventually, the cracks started to show. He couldn't keep up the version of himself that wasn't real. And he started to unravel.

That's when the lies came up, one by one, like splinters that had been lodged under his skin for years.

I'm only loved when I perform.

If I stop trying so hard, people will leave.

I can't show weakness—it makes me unworthy.

I'm not worth choosing.

He didn't realize how much power those lies held until he started naming them out loud.

And then... something shifted.

Truth didn't shout at him. It didn't demand he fix everything overnight.

It whispered. It invited. It waited.

He remembers reading a verse one morning— *"You are fearfully and wonderfully made."*

He almost skipped past it. It felt like a verse for someone else. Someone better. Someone... cleaner.

But something in him paused.

What if... just what if... that could be true for him, too?

He began the long, holy work of unlearning.

It meant catching the internal voice that said, *"You're a failure,"* and asking, *"Says who?"*

It meant stopping mid-thought to rewrite the script:

"No, I'm not too much. I'm learning how to be honest."

"No, I'm not unworthy. I'm healing."

There were relapses, of course. Days when the old lies sounded louder than the new truths.

But with each step, he got better at recognizing the difference.

Lies shame you into silence. Truth sets you free to speak.

Lies demand performance. Truth invites presence.

Lies bind. Truth breaks chains.

Micah still wrestles sometimes. He still feels the sting of old beliefs sneak in when he's tired or vulnerable. But now, he's not defenseless.

He's learning to hold space for the younger version of himself who didn't know better—who was just trying to survive.

And he's learning to speak gently to the current version of himself, the one still becoming.

He doesn't pretend anymore. He doesn't shrink. He doesn't need to.

He's no longer living to silence the lies. He's living to speak the truth.

Not just with his words—but with his life.

"She is clothed with strength and dignity;
she can laugh at the days to come."

Proverbs 31:25 (NIV)

Chapter 14:

To the Moments I Forgot to Laugh

Dear Me (The One Who Forgot Joy),

There was a time you thought laughter was a luxury.

Like it had to be earned. Like it didn't belong in the middle of grief.

You forgot for a while—but you found it again. And when you did, it didn't fix everything.

It just reminded you that not everything was broken.

You're allowed to laugh. Even in the middle. Even when you're not okay.

That kind of joy? It's not denial.

It's survival.

Keep laughing.

Even if it's through tears.

—Micah

Micah remembered the night his daughter put socks on her hands and danced to '80s music in the kitchen. It had been one of *those* weeks—emotionally heavy, spiritually silent, the kind where every breath felt like work. He had barely spoken all day, carrying the weight of too many thoughts that had no names.

But there she was. A blur of chaotic joy, arms flailing, giggling as she slid across the floor in mismatched pajamas.

"Look, I'm a sock monster!" she yelled with pride, fingers poking through pink fuzzy fabric.

And just like that—he cracked.

Not a forced grin. Not the tired smirk he'd mastered over the years to keep people at ease.

He *laughed*.

A laugh that came from deep in his gut, from some long-sealed room that hadn't seen daylight in ages. It bubbled up without permission. It was messy and loud and unpolished. It didn't ask if the moment was appropriate.

He laughed until he couldn't breathe.

And for once, the tears in his eyes weren't born of sadness. That night, something shifted.

He didn't walk away healed. But he walked away reminded.

Joy wasn't the reward at the end of healing. It was part of the journey.

Micah had once believed that if he laughed too soon, he was being dishonest. That if he smiled while still hurting, he was betraying the pain.

But that night taught him something sacred:

Laughter doesn't erase grief. It balances it.

There was still a long road ahead. But suddenly, that road didn't feel quite as dark.

He started collecting those moments. Not with a camera, not for social media—just for him. For the memory shelf he kept inside, the one labeled *proof I'm still alive.*

There was the night his son told a knock-knock joke that made absolutely no sense—but Micah laughed anyway because his son's grin was brighter than the punchline.

There was the group chat where someone shared a poorly drawn dinosaur meme that made him wheeze-laugh into his coffee.

There was the random day when he wore two different shoes to work and didn't even notice until lunch. He didn't curse. He didn't spiral. He laughed.

Then there was the time he dropped an entire box of cereal in the grocery store aisle. A younger version of him might've panicked, flushed red, felt small.

But this time, he knelt to clean it up and said, "Welp, guess I'm starting a new trend. Floor flakes."

And a stranger chuckled with him. That felt like winning.

Micah came to see laughter as its own kind of resilience.

It wasn't just a reaction.

It was an act of defiance.

To laugh was to say, *I'm still here.*

To laugh was to claim space in a world that had tried to push him into silence.

To laugh was to remember that even in the middle of the mess, he was still human.

He didn't laugh every day. Some days were still quiet. Some days were heavy.

But the laughter came easier now. And what surprised him most was that it wasn't always earned.

Sometimes it just arrived. And instead of pushing it away, he let it stay.

He learned to stop apologizing for joy.

Learned that you don't have to wait until the storm is over to dance. Sometimes the lightning becomes part of the rhythm.

There were still hard days ahead. Healing wasn't a straight line, and Micah knew that.

But in between the journal entries and therapy sessions and deep soul work—there was a sacred kind of lightness.

Laughter didn't save him. But it reminded him that he was worth saving.

And that… was enough.

"We love because He first loved us"

1 John 4:19 (NIV)

Chapter 15:

To the First Time I Felt Love

Dear Me (The First Time),

You were terrified, weren't you?

Terrified you'd mess it up. Terrified you wouldn't be enough. Terrified that all the pain you carried would find a way to bleed into her life.

But then she arrived.

And in a moment that split your heart wide open, you realized something that words couldn't explain:

This is love. Not the kind you chased. Not the kind you lost. But the kind that chooses you back, before you even know how to be chosen.

You didn't have to earn it.

You just had to receive it.

She made you a father. But more than that—she made you feel for the first time.

—Micah

Micah had never known a love that didn't require performance.

He had always believed love was something earned—through good behavior, through pleasing others, through silence and survival. He had tried on so many masks, convinced that one of them might make him lovable. He'd been a son, a soldier, a partner—each role layered with the silent prayer: *Please let this be enough.*

And then… came her.

It wasn't the pregnancy test or the doctor's confirmation that shook him—it was the weight of holding his daughter for the first time.

She didn't speak. She didn't smile. She didn't do anything except *exist.*

And yet, she undid him.

Her cry wasn't loud, but it was enough to split something inside him. He watched her tiny chest rise and fall in sync with life itself. Her fingers curled instinctively around his thumb as if to say, *You're mine. And I'm yours.*

He'd never felt more seen—or more responsible—in his entire life.

Micah had feared fatherhood. He was haunted by questions no one could answer:

Would I repeat the mistakes of those before me? Would I hurt her like I had been hurt? Would I be enough?

He remembered pacing the hospital room in the early hours, the pale fluorescent light casting long shadows on the walls. He wasn't pacing because of anxiety—he was pacing because something inside him was *awakening*. Something primal. Something sacred.

This little girl, wrapped in a hospital blanket, didn't care about his past.

She didn't ask him to be fixed. She didn't flinch when she looked at him. She simply trusted.

And that trust cracked open every wall he had built around his heart.

For the first time in his life, Micah didn't have to prove he was lovable—he just was. Her love wasn't earned. It was innate. And it called something forward in him that had been buried under years of silence, shame, and self-doubt.

He didn't know what kind of father he'd be. He didn't have a perfect example. But in that moment, he made a quiet vow—not a vow to be flawless, but to show up.

Every day.

Every night.

Even when he was tired.

Even when he was afraid.

He vowed to love her, not through grand gestures or impossible standards, but through *presence*.

There were sleepless nights that tested him. Crying fits that frayed his nerves. Diapers and bottles and the mental weight of wondering if he was doing anything right.

But there were also giggles at 3 AM. Tiny fingers tangled in his beard. Eyes that lit up when he walked into the room.

She didn't care if he got it all right. She just wanted him.

Micah realized that love wasn't about fixing someone else—or being fixed.

It wasn't about perfect timing or perfect words. It was about *being there*. It was about *choosing to stay*.

As his daughter grew, so did he.

She became his mirror. In her, he saw the gentler parts of himself—the parts that hadn't been hardened by disappointment. She reminded him that tenderness wasn't weakness. That vulnerability was brave. That love, when rooted in grace, could heal generations.

And though he still struggled—still faced days when old voices whispered lies about his worth—her presence remained a constant truth.

He remembered one night, rocking her to sleep after a hard day. She nestled into his chest, sighing the way only babies can— like the world was completely safe in his arms. He closed his eyes and realized:

This… this is the safest I've ever felt too.

Micah didn't find redemption in becoming a father.

He found *invitation*. An invitation to love without fear.

To feel without hiding.

To give without expecting.

To receive without guilt.

His daughter didn't save him. She didn't have to. She simply showed up—and in doing so, gave him the courage to do the same.

So when people ask when he first felt love—not the fleeting kind, not the conditional kind, but the real kind—he doesn't hesitate.

It wasn't a wedding. It wasn't a kiss. It wasn't a mountaintop moment.

It was in a hospital room, under dull lights, with a crying newborn pressed against his chest.

And in that moment, Micah's heart, after years of hiding, *finally opened.*

Not because someone told him he was worthy. But because *she believed it*—before he ever said a word.

"The human spirit is stronger than anything that can happen to it."

—C.C. Scott

Chapter 16:

To the Version of Me Who Survived

Dear Me (The Survivor),

You never thought you'd make it out.

You didn't think you were strong enough. But you kept going. And that's the greatest victory of all.

Your scars? They're not shame. They're proof that you lived. Proof that you endured.

Proof that you're still here, still standing, still choosing to fight for yourself.

Don't ever forget how much strength it took to keep going.

Don't you ever forget who you are.

—Micah

Micah had never liked the word. It felt too big. Too dramatic. It was a title he thought belonged to people who had lived through war zones or natural disasters, who had stared death in the face and walked away with nothing but dust in their lungs and fire in their eyes.

He didn't feel like that.

He felt... tired.

Worn down by a thousand quiet battles no one ever saw. Haunted by wounds that didn't bleed but still left him gasping. He had spent most of his life minimizing his pain, telling himself others had it worse, convincing himself that what he went through didn't count as survival.

But the truth?

It did.

He had survived the slow erosion of self-worth. He had survived abandonment and shame.

He had survived the kind of loneliness that wraps itself around your ribcage and convinces you no one would notice if you disappeared.

He had survived himself. And that—*that*—was worth honoring.

There was a time when Micah didn't think he'd make it.

Not just through a hard season or a difficult year, but t*hrough life itself.*

He remembered the nights when the silence was deafening, when even the sound of his own heartbeat felt like a burden. Nights when the weight of everything unspoken pressed down so hard he wondered if it would ever lift.

But somehow, he kept going. Not always because he was brave. Sometimes just because he didn't know what else to do.

He got out of bed when he didn't want to. He showed up to life even when he felt hollow. He smiled when it hurt. He gave when he was empty.

That's survival, too.

The world often celebrates the dramatic comebacks, the obvious victories—the addict who gets clean, the patient who beats the diagnosis, the runaway who returns home. But no one talks about the quiet survivors. The ones who hold their breath just to get through the day. The ones who wake up to the same pain again and again and *still* choose to face it.

Micah was one of those survivors. His trauma didn't make the headlines. But it shaped him all the same.

The childhood rejection. The buried grief. The weight of being misunderstood. The relationships that unraveled because he didn't yet know how to hold himself together. The years of pretending, performing, hiding.

It all left its mark. But it didn't win.

Because somewhere along the way, Micah made a choice—not a loud, cinematic choice, but a quiet, defiant one:

To live.

He didn't fully understand what that meant at the time. Living didn't mean pretending to be happy. It didn't mean faking his way through life. It meant staying. Showing up. Asking hard questions. Feeling pain he had avoided for years. Letting people in, even when it scared him.

Healing didn't come like a flood. It came like a drip.

Small moments. Small shifts. Small choices.

A therapy session where he told the truth for the first time.

A phone call he didn't hang up on.

A mirror he looked into and said, "You're still here."

Each moment was a thread. And over time, Micah wove those threads into something strong enough to hold him.

He stopped seeing his past as a curse and started seeing it as context.

He stopped apologizing for his scars and started honoring them.

He stopped asking, *Why me?* and started asking, *What now?*

Survival wasn't about what he escaped. It was about who he became because of it. He became someone who could sit with pain without running.

Someone who could feel everything—and not be undone by it. Someone who could love others without losing himself in the process.

He became *whole*.

Not perfect. Not finished. But whole. That wholeness didn't mean the past disappeared. It meant the past no longer defined him.

Micah had finally learned that survival wasn't a moment—it was a posture. A commitment to rise again, even when the fall had been brutal. A belief that hope is still worth holding, even with trembling hands.

So now, when he looks in the mirror, he doesn't just see the version of himself he's become—he sees all the versions that got him here.

The boy who cried in secret. The teenager who begged for acceptance. The soldier who wore strength like armor. The husband who tried and failed. The father who learned to feel.

The man who stood in the rubble of his life and *built something new.*

Micah finally understood: He didn't survive despite the pain. He survived *through* it.

And now?

Now, he lives.

"Come to me, all who are weary and burdened, and I will give you rest"

Matthew 11:28 (NIV)

Chapter 17:

To the One Who Tried to Be God

Dear Me (The One Who Tried to Be God),

You meant well. You were trying to keep everyone safe. To hold it all together. To make sure no one ever saw you fall apart.

But you were never meant to carry it all.

You don't have to be the savior. You don't have to be the strong one all the time. You don't have to fix what only grace can heal.

Let go.

Not because you're weak. But because you were never supposed to do this alone.

—Micah

Micah didn't set out to try and be God. That wasn't the plan. He didn't wake up one morning and declare himself the almighty fixer of the universe. No—he just wanted to help. He wanted to make things right.

He thought he was just being responsible—doing what had to be done. He believed that if he worked hard enough, cared deep enough, tried long enough, he could hold everything together. His marriage. His kids. His story. His mind.

But slowly, the weight of it all began to crush him.

He had grown up in chaos—emotionally, spiritually, relationally. So when adulthood came, he clung to control like a life vest. Control meant safety. Control meant predictability. It meant never feeling that helpless again.

So he built routines and checklists and backup plans. He scheduled his life down to the minute. He anticipated everyone's needs before they could speak them. If something broke, he fixed it. If someone hurt, he patched it. If something went wrong, he owned it—even when it wasn't his to carry.

He became the anchor for everyone else.

But being everyone's anchor meant he was constantly sinking.

The world called it strength. His friends admired his steadiness. His coworkers praised his leadership. Even his family leaned on him without ever realizing how much it cost him.

But deep down, Micah knew the truth.

It wasn't strength. It was fear in a tailored disguise.

It was the fear of being out of control. The fear of disappointing people. The fear that if he let go, even for a second, everything would fall apart—and the blame would land squarely on his shoulders.

He didn't know how to rest.

Even on his days off, his mind didn't stop spinning—checking, planning, calculating. When his phone buzzed, his heart rate jumped. When someone asked, "Can we talk?" his stomach turned with anxiety. He wore calm like a costume, but underneath it, he was unraveling.

He prayed, but not from a place of trust. It was more like a transaction. "God, I'll keep doing everything I can… and maybe You'll show up and fill in the gaps." But what he never said out loud—what he barely admitted to himself—was this:

He didn't trust that God would show up.

So he took over. He filled the silence with noise. He filled the stillness with movement. He filled the unknown with effort.

He wouldn't have called it playing God. But when you believe the outcome depends solely on you, isn't that exactly what you're doing?

One Tuesday afternoon, the weight finally buckled.

Micah sat in his car outside the grocery store, keys in the ignition, engine running, but he couldn't move. His chest was tight, his breathing shallow. His hands trembled on the steering wheel. It wasn't just one thing—it was everything.

The arguments. The unmet expectations. The endless responsibilities. The silent ache in his soul that said, "You're not enough," no matter how much he did.

Tears welled up unexpectedly. Not gentle, poetic tears. But a wave of grief and exhaustion and fury that had nowhere else to go.

"I can't do this anymore."

It wasn't a breakdown. It was a breakthrough.

He walked into the house, found his wife in the kitchen, and told her the truth. Not the cleaned-up version. The raw, trembling, mascara-staining kind of truth. He cried in her arms like a child, finally admitting the thing he'd buried for years:

"I'm tired of being the strong one."

She didn't fix it. She just held him. And for the first time in a long time… he let her.

That night, Micah picked up his journal—the same one he used to write in every day but had abandoned somewhere between trying to be perfect and trying to survive. He wrote the words, "I don't know who I am if I'm not fixing everything."

And slowly, a new journey began.

He started therapy. He stopped saying yes to things just because he was afraid of being seen as selfish. He began trusting others with pieces of his heart, even when it felt risky.

And through that process, Micah began to believe what grace had been whispering to him all along:

You don't have to be God to be good. You don't have to save the world to matter in it. You don't have to prove your worth through exhaustion.

Strength wasn't pretending. Strength was telling the truth.

Strength was resting even when the to-do list wasn't done. Strength was letting others carry you when your knees gave out. Strength was letting go—not because everything was okay—but because you finally trusted that *you* didn't have to be the one to make it okay.

Micah still wrestled with the urge to over-function. But now he recognized the signs. Now he could pause and ask, "Am I trying to play God again?"

More often than not, the answer was yes. And more often than not, he chose to let go anyway.

Micah found freedom—not in control, but in surrender. Not in performance, but in grace. Not in being everyone's savior, but in trusting the One who already was.

And for the first time in a long time...

He could breathe.

"Love isn't about finding someone to complete you.
It's about finding someone who reminds you,
you were already whole."

—*Unknown*

Chapter 18:

To the One I Was Always Meant to Find

Dear Me (The One Who Was Always Meant to Find),

You were searching for her, weren't you?

Searching for someone who could quiet the storm inside.

You thought she could heal your wounds. You thought she was the missing piece—the one who could finally make everything feel right.

But the truth?

She was never meant to fix you. She was meant to walk with you. She wasn't your salvation. She was your partner.

And for that, I am grateful.

You didn't need to find her to be complete. You needed to find yourself first.

And that, my friend, is the real love story.

—Micah

Micah had spent much of his life in pursuit of a person he didn't even know how to describe—only that he believed she existed. Somewhere out there was her. The one who would make him feel safe. The one who would make him feel whole. The one who would take away the ache that had followed him for as long as he could remember.

He called it love.

But in hindsight, it had been longing—disguised as romance.

It wasn't until later that he realized how often he had mistaken need for love, dependence for connection, fantasy for future.

Then came Jenna.

And with her, everything changed—not because she completed him, but because she *didn't*.

She met him at a point in his life where he was no longer searching for a savior. He had already begun the painful, necessary work of healing. He had stopped looking for someone to rescue him and had started becoming someone who could finally stand on his own two feet.

That's when she entered the story—not as a cure, but as a *companion*.

Jenna was strong and steady. Soft, but not timid. She didn't need Micah to perform for her. She didn't fall for a façade. She loved him without needing him to prove himself.

And that, more than anything, terrified him.

Because real love—*healthy* love—meant he had to show up fully. Not partially. Not selectively. But completely.

Jenna didn't see a man who had it all figured out. She saw a man who had been wounded and was still learning to heal. She saw a father trying his best. A husband trying to get it right this time. A soul that had known the weight of silence and was learning how to speak.

She didn't idolize him. She didn't romanticize his past. She simply *chose* him.

Every day.

And for Micah, that kind of consistent, grounded love was revolutionary.

They built something slowly. Intentionally. With honesty at the center. There were no games. No pretending. No illusions of perfection. Just two people, standing face to face, saying, "I want to walk this road with you, flaws and all."

There were hard days. Moments of miscommunication. Old wounds that still sometimes whispered. But they didn't run. They didn't retreat into silence or shame. They leaned in.

They learned to fight *with* each other, not against each other.

Jenna wasn't impressed by Micah's masks. She didn't want the "best version" of him—she wanted the real one. And slowly, he began to believe that version of himself was enough.

Through her, he discovered that the greatest kind of love doesn't demand perfection.

It offers *presence*.

Micah used to think love meant losing yourself in someone else.

Now he knew—real love means being fully yourself and still being *fully loved*.

Jenna gave him that. She never promised to heal his past. But she stood beside him as he confronted it.

She didn't hold his hand through everything—sometimes, she simply stood near, letting him know he wasn't alone.

And that was enough.

Micah had once believed that love was the end of the story—the final chapter where everything falls into place. But with Jenna, he realized that love is the *beginning*.

The beginning of doing life together.

Of choosing honesty over ease. Of learning each other, again and again. Of becoming, not just loving.

What they built was not built on fantasies. It was built on friendship. On faith. On trust.

And, most importantly, it was built on a truth Micah had fought for years to accept *he was worthy of love—just as he was*.

Jenna didn't complete him. She *confirmed* what he had finally come to believe:

That love is not something you earn.

It's something you receive, when you're ready to stop hiding.

That love doesn't save you. It meets you.

And when it does—it doesn't come with fireworks. It comes with peace. With stillness.

With knowing you can finally *breathe*.

*"The righteous man walks in his integrity;
his children are blessed after him."*

Proverbs 20:17 (NIV)

Chapter 19:

To the Father I'm Still Becoming

Dear Me (The Father),

You're not perfect—and you never will be. But you're trying. And that's more than enough.

You'll mess up. You'll stumble. You'll say the wrong thing. You'll lose your temper. You'll lie awake at night wondering if you're doing any of it right.

But your kids?

They won't remember all your mistakes. They'll remember that you showed up. That you were there when it mattered. That you kept coming back, even when it was hard.

That's what matters. That's the real legacy.

Keep going. Keep growing.

You are becoming the father they need—not because you're perfect, but because you're present.

—Micah

Becoming a father was never part of Micah's five-year plan.

He wasn't prepared. Emotionally, financially, spiritually—he didn't feel ready in any sense of the word. He had spent most of his life trying to piece himself back together, still unsure if the man he was becoming could be trusted to raise another.

But when his son, Jonah, was placed in his arms for the first time, the world went silent.

There was no dramatic music. No cinematic montage. Just stillness.

And in that stillness, *everything changed*.

Jonah's eyes blinked up at him, wide and unaware. His fingers flexed and curled, reaching instinctively for something—any-thing—to hold onto.

Micah had spent decades wondering where he belonged.

Now he knew *right here*.

At first, the fear was paralyzing.

Micah had so many unanswered questions. What if he passed on his pain? What if he messed up like others had messed up before him? What if love alone wasn't enough?

He didn't have a blueprint. He hadn't grown up with a clear picture of what a present, engaged, emotionally available father looked like. So much of his parenting began from scratch—built not on inheritance, but on *intention*.

He didn't always know what to say. He didn't always know what to do. But he made a promise in those early days:

Show up.

And he did.

Through late-night feedings and diaper blowouts. Through toddler tantrums and scraped knees. Through quiet moments in the hallway when Jonah couldn't sleep, and Micah held him tight, whispering, "I've got you."

And slowly, Micah began to believe it—*he did have this.*

Not because he was doing everything right, but because he was *trying.*

He learned that kids don't need perfect fathers. They need *safe* ones. They need someone who shows up even when he's tired.

Someone who apologizes when he gets it wrong. Someone who models honesty, growth, and grace.

Micah began to see fatherhood not as a task to master, but as a *relationship to nurture.*

He didn't have to have all the answers. He just had to stay present long enough to help Jonah ask the right questions.

And with each child that followed—each new little voice calling him "Dad"—Micah's heart stretched further. Not perfectly, not painlessly, but powerfully.

There were days when it all felt like too much.

When he was juggling bills, work stress, exhaustion, and the lingering ache of wounds he thought were long gone.

There were days when his temper ran short. When his patience frayed. When he caught himself reacting instead of responding.

Those were the nights he sat outside their bedrooms and prayed silently: *God, help me be better tomorrow.*

But there were also moments—so many moments—that reminded him why it all mattered.

The spontaneous hugs. The bedtime "I love yous." The drawings labeled "Daddy" in crooked handwriting.

The first time Jonah asked him, "Are you proud of me?"—and Micah didn't just say yes. He meant it.

Micah saw the full circle. He had once been a boy asking the world if he was enough.

Now, he was raising a generation who *would never have to wonder.*

That was his greatest calling. Not to be perfect. But to *break the cycle.*

To raise his kids in an environment where emotion wasn't weakness, where questions were welcome, where failure wasn't final, and where love was never earned—it was freely given.

The title "Dad" didn't make Micah feel powerful. It made him feel *responsible.*

Not to fix everything, but to be the kind of man his children could trust—*not just admire from a distance.*

He didn't want to be the hero in their stories. He wanted to be the *anchor.* The one they could count on. Cry to. Come home to.

And as the years passed, Micah began to embrace something beautiful:

He wasn't just raising children. He was becoming someone worth being raised by.

Fatherhood wasn't the end of his story. It was the *redemption* of it.

A daily invitation to become the man he had always needed. A daily reminder that love—real, patient, steady love—was enough.

So, no—Micah wasn't a perfect father. But he was a present one.

And that made all the difference.

"Fathers, do not provoke your children to anger,
but bring them up in the discipline
and instruction of the Lord."

Ephesians 6:4 (NIV)

Chapter 20:

To the Daughter Who Made Me Soft

Dear Daughter (The One Who Made Me Soft),

I didn't know I could love like this. Not until you.

You came into my life like a sunrise—quiet, steady, unstoppable.

And from the first time I held you, something in me broke open in the best possible way. Not broken like damage.

Broken like soil—ready, finally, to grow something good.

You didn't ask me to be perfect. You just asked me to be there.

And somehow, that made me want to become the kind of man you'd be proud to run to when the world got loud.

You gave me a second chance—not just at fatherhood, but at being human. At being present. At being soft in a world that taught me to be hard.

When I look at you, I see everything I want to protect—your kindness, your spark, your questions, your belly laughs that echo through the house like joy forgot how to whisper.

I see the little girl who dances in socks across the kitchen floor. I see the teenager you'll become—eyes wide with wonder and fire. I see the woman I'll one day send out into the world, hoping she never forgets her worth.

But most of all, I see me—the version of me I didn't know still existed.

The one who believes love is worth the risk. The one who cries at bedtime prayers and clutches drawings with "I love you, Daddy" scrawled across the top.

I want you to know something, baby girl: You didn't just make me a father. You made me better.

You softened my sharp edges. You slowed my anxious pace. You taught me that real strength isn't about never bending—it's about choosing love, again and again, no matter how tired the day.

So when the world tries to tell you that you're too much or not enough—

Remember this: You are fiercely, wildly, wonderfully loved.

Not because of what you do. Not because of how well you behave.

But because you're mine. And more than that—because you're you.

I'll never stop cheering for you. I'll never stop learning from you. And I'll never stop thanking God for the day He gave me the gift of being your dad.

Always,
—Dad

Micah hadn't expected her to undo him.

He thought he would be the protector. The steady one. The teacher.

But then she came—tiny, loud, full of wonder—and turned his world into something far more sacred than he'd ever imagined.

She didn't just change his schedule. She changed him.

There was something about the way she looked at him, like he was still good. Still capable. Still worthy of being loved, even when he didn't feel like he deserved it.

Her love wasn't earned. It was simply given.

She called him Daddy like it was the safest word in her vocabulary. And somehow, every time she said it, something in him healed.

Micah found himself crying more since she was born—not out of sadness, but out of a tenderness he hadn't known how to access before.

He cried watching her dance barefoot in the living room, twirling in a world that hadn't yet tried to shrink her.

He cried when she brought him a crayon drawing of the two of them holding hands under a sky full of uneven hearts.

He cried when she climbed into his lap during his hardest week and whispered, "I just want to be where you are."

He'd spent most of his life trying to be strong. Trying to be enough. Trying to hide the parts of himself that felt broken.

But she didn't need a strong man. She needed a *present* one.

She needed someone to notice when her voice trembled. Someone to kneel—not just to her height, but to her *world*. Someone who didn't always have the answers but always had time.

And that's what Micah decided he would be. Not a perfect dad. But a safe one.

One who says, "I'm sorry" when he gets it wrong. One who says, "I'm proud of you" for more than just accomplishments. One who holds space for her tears instead of rushing to fix them.

Because he remembered what it felt like to have no one meet him there.

To cry alone. To question his worth. To search for approval in a world that only rewarded performance.

He didn't want that story for her.

He wanted her to know—deep in her bones—that she didn't have to earn her place in the world.

That her voice mattered. That her emotions weren't too much. That her softness was strength.

Micah watched her grow—watched her curiosity bloom, her empathy deepen, her confidence flicker and return.

And every step felt like an invitation to show up better than the man he used to be.

Sometimes he failed.

Sometimes he raised his voice.

Sometimes he let the weight of the day dull his tone or distract his mind.

But he always came back. Always circled back to her room, her heart, her face—

To remind her that love doesn't leave.

That love apologizes.

That love *stays*.

And in those moments, Micah realized something he hadn't understood before:

She wasn't just his daughter. She was a mirror.

She reflected back the boy he used to be—the one who needed softness but only knew survival. She gave him the courage to rewrite that story. Not by erasing it, but by choosing a better ending.

Now, every time she laughs,

Every time she falls asleep mid-sentence,

Every time she grabs his hand just because—

Micah feels the echo of grace.

She made him soft.

And in a world that told him softness was weakness,

She taught him it was strength.

Micah didn't save her.

She saved him too.

*"Train up a child in the way he should go;
even when he is old, he will not depart from it."*

Proverbs 22:6 (NIV)

Chapter 21:

To the Sons I'm Learning to Raise

Dear Sons (Still Becoming),

I don't have all the answers. I wish I did.

Some days, I wish I could wrap you in certainty and shield you from every scar. But that's not how this works.

What I can give you is presence. What I can offer is truth. What I can promise is that I'll never stop trying to be the man I want you to become.

You won't always see me get it right. But I hope you'll always see me try.

And when you reach the places in your life where things fall apart, where the world feels too heavy, I pray you'll remember this:

You are not what you do. You are not how well you perform. You are not too much, and you are never not enough.

You are loved. You are mine. And even more than that—you are His.

I'm learning how to raise you as I learn how to heal. We're growing up together.

—Dad

Micah never imagined he'd have sons.

And when he did, he didn't realize how much of himself he'd see in their eyes.

Not just in their laughter or the way they walked, but in their fears. In their questions. In their softness.

He wasn't ready for how it would all come back. How holding his son's hand would somehow hold the hand of the boy he used to be. How raising a child would stir every place he had been abandoned, misunderstood, or unseen.

Micah was determined to be a better man than the one who left him. Determined to write a new story.

But some days, that meant wrestling ghosts he didn't know were still hiding in him.

He found himself afraid of repeating what hurt him. Afraid of being too harsh. Too distant. Too wrapped up in his own healing to offer the kind of guidance his boys would need.

But they didn't need perfection. They just needed him. Not the fixed version. The present one.

Micah learned that sometimes, love looks like sitting on the floor surrounded by Legos after a long day.

Sometimes it sounds like "I'm sorry" whispered after raising your voice too quickly. Sometimes it looks like listening to stories that don't make sense just to show that their voice matters.

He started to understand that fatherhood wasn't a performance—it was proximity.

And legacy wasn't built in big, Instagrammable moments. It was built in the way he looked at them. The way he knelt instead of shouted. The way he owned his mistakes instead of hiding them.

One night, his youngest son came to him with tears in his eyes. "I feel like I mess up everything," he whispered.

Micah's heart broke open. Because that sentence had lived in his chest for years.

He pulled him close, ran his fingers through his hair, and said the words he had always needed someone to say: "It's okay to mess up. It doesn't change who you are. You're still good. You're still mine."

That night, Micah cried after his son fell asleep. Not because he was sad—but because he finally understood something holy: Healing doesn't just come from what you receive.

Sometimes it comes from what you give back.

Micah was raising sons—but he was also raising the part of himself that had been forgotten.

He watched them run, unafraid. He listened to their endless questions and saw curiosity instead of rebellion. He saw their big emotions not as disrespect, but as undeveloped strength.

They weren't too much. They were becoming.

And in raising them, Micah began to let go of the shame he'd carried for so long.

He stopped demanding perfection of himself. Stopped measuring his worth by how calm he stayed or how successful he looked. He just started being *Dad*.

Present. Imperfect. Loving.

There were hard days. Tantrums, exhaustion, discipline, disappointment. There were moments when he didn't know what to do—so he prayed. Not polished prayers. But raw, messy ones.

"God, help me not repeat what I've seen. Help me give them what I didn't get. Help me raise men who don't have to unlearn love."

And God answered. Not with ease—but with grace.

Grace that met Micah when he failed. Grace that whispered, "try again." Grace that reminded him that even when he was struggling, he was still the right father for them.

He learned that strength isn't stoicism—it's presence. That leadership isn't control—it's compassion. That legacy isn't what you leave behind—it's who you walk beside.

Micah didn't always know what he was doing.

But he kept showing up.

And that was enough.

Now, when he looks at his sons, he doesn't just see who they are—he sees who they're becoming. He sees the kind of men they might be.

And it makes him fight a little harder to become the kind of man they can look up to—not for perfection, but for honesty.

Micah is still learning. Still growing. Still breaking old patterns and building new foundations.

But he's not doing it alone.

Because in the laughter, in the chaos, in the bedtime prayers and morning hugs—something sacred is happening.

Micah isn't just raising sons. He's raising healing. He's raising hope. He's raising the future.

And he's grateful. For every moment. Every mess. Every question.

Because fatherhood didn't just change his life. It gave his story a new ending.

One filled with love.

One rooted in redemption.

One he can finally be proud to pass on.

*"The light shines in the darkness,
and the darkness has not overcome it."*

John 1:5 (NIV)

Chapter 22:

To the Nights I Didn't Want to Wake Up

Dear Me (In the Dark),

You didn't want to die. You just didn't know how to keep living.

You were exhausted—not in the way a nap could fix, but in the way that made your soul ache. You were drowning beneath a smile, buried under the weight of pretending everything was fine.

It wasn't that you hated life. You just couldn't find your place in it anymore.

You tried. God, you tried. You prayed, journaled, worshiped, pushed yourself to smile, kept showing up. And still, the nights grew darker.

I wish I could go back there—to that room, that silence, that breath you almost didn't take—and just sit beside you. No sermons. No quick fixes. I wouldn't tell you to "have faith" or "be strong." I'd just be there. Present. Quiet.

And I'd whisper what you couldn't believe back then: Even now…Even here…You matter.

You always did. I'm so proud you stayed.

—Micah

Micah had always been the strong one.

He didn't sign up for it. He just inherited it—this unspoken expectation to carry the weight for others. He was the safe place, the encourager, the "you can do this" guy. The dependable one. The shoulder to cry on.

But when you're always holding others up, no one thinks to ask how heavy you're feeling.

It started quietly.

He couldn't pinpoint the exact day things shifted. It was more like a slow fade—colors draining from life. Laughter lost its echo. Hope felt like a stranger. Sleep came in pieces, and peace felt like a lie.

It wasn't one thing. It was everything.

Old wounds reopened. Disappointments stacked like bricks on his chest. Grief that had gone unspoken for years started to scream. The weight of fatherhood, faith, failure, shame, and exhaustion collapsed on him like a storm he couldn't escape.

He told himself it would pass. That he just needed a break. That he was just tired.

But the tired didn't end.

He became a ghost in his own life—functioning, present, but hollow. He kissed his kids goodnight with a smile that didn't quite reach his eyes.

He held his wife while silently wondering if she'd be better off without him. He preached hope to others and went home feeling like a fraud.

There was a stillness in him that wasn't peace. It was apathy.

He didn't want to *die*. Not really. He just didn't want to *wake up*.

The mornings became the hardest part—waking up to the same weight, the same ache, the same "how am I still here?"

He stopped dreaming about the future. Stopped making plans. Stopped believing tomorrow could hold anything different than today.

And worst of all... He kept it all to himself.

Because how do you say out loud, "I think I'm disappearing"?

How do you explain that you feel like a burden even to the people who love you most?

How do you admit that faith feels distant, God feels silent, and prayer feels like a voicemail left on an empty line?

He knew the scriptures. He knew the truths. He had been the one to remind others of God's promises.

But when your soul is hemorrhaging, verses feel like band-aids.

There was one night—colder than the rest. The house was silent, everyone asleep. Micah sat on the edge of the bathtub, a towel in his lap like it could somehow anchor him to the world.

And he just stared.

No tears. No drama. Just... blank. Exhausted beyond words.

And that's when it came.

A whisper. Not from outside, but from the very depths of his soul—buried beneath the pain, beneath the numbness.

"Stay."

It wasn't a command. It was an invitation. Stay.

Not because it would get easier right away. Not because he had answers. Not because he deserved to.

Just stay. Because maybe surviving the night was enough.

He sat there for what felt like hours. Breathing. Not planning. Not fixing. Just being. Still. Alive.

And in the morning, he did the next brave thing: He told someone.

A text, five words long: **"I don't want to be here."**

He expected silence. Or maybe judgment. But his friend responded in the most powerful way possible: he came. No clichés. No sermons. Just presence. And Micah wept.

For the first time in months, he let the tears fall.

That was the turning point—not the moment he was "healed," but the moment he stopped pretending he wasn't broken.

He started therapy. Started journaling again. Started talking— really talking—to his wife.

He stopped apologizing for his pain. Stopped explaining it away. Stopped believing the lie that struggling made him weak.

He learned to ask for help.

He relearned how to breathe. How to grieve. How to exist without performing. How to be Micah—even when Micah wasn't "okay."

There were still hard nights. Still shadows. Still moments when the dark crept in. But now, he wasn't alone in it.

He built a community—not of perfect people, but of honest ones. People who could say, "Me too." People who didn't flinch at his story.

And slowly, the light returned. Not all at once. Not in a cinematic burst. But in glimmers.

His daughter's laughter. His wife's prayers. The soft warmth of coffee in the morning. The quiet worship song that caught him off guard. The journal entry that didn't end in despair.

Micah began to hope again—not the kind of hope that says everything will be perfect, but the kind that says it's worth staying for the story that isn't over yet.

He started to see the sacredness of survival. The bravery of just showing up. The power of saying, "I'm still here."

Because there's nothing weak about fighting invisible battles. There's nothing shameful about needing help. There's nothing broken about feeling broken.

He learned that you don't have to want to live forever. You just have to live *today*.

And when someone else reaches out—whispering the same fear Micah once carried—he knows what to say.

Not "cheer up."

Not "just pray harder."

Not "God won't give you more than you can handle."

He leans in, voice steady, heart open. And says,

"Stay. I'm so glad I did."

Because Micah's story didn't end on the bathroom floor. That was where it began again.

"Stay. You don't have to know how to fix it. You just have to stay. I'm so glad I did."

*"God has not called us to go to church.
He has called us to be His church."*

—Unknown

Chapter 23:

To the Church That Broke Me

Dear Church (That Was Supposed to Be Home),

You were meant to be the safest place. A refuge. A family. A hospital for the hurting.

But I walked in with wounds and walked out with more. You didn't mean to. Most of you were just doing what you were taught. Rules over relationship. Performance over presence. Clean over real.

But your silence cut deeper than the world's noise. Your judgment hit harder than the world's rejection. And your love—when it came with conditions—felt more like a leash than a lifeline.

Still, I don't hate you. I grieved you. I wrestled with you. And somehow, I still believe in the beauty you were meant to hold.

But first—I had to name what you became.

You hurt me. But you didn't get to keep me.

—Micah

Micah didn't walk away from God. He walked away from the place that claimed to represent Him.

The difference was everything. But it took him years to see it.

At first, he thought the problem was him. He wasn't "on fire" enough. Didn't raise his hands high enough. Didn't cry during the altar calls.

He sat quietly with doubts and shame and unspoken trauma—and learned to translate that silence into guilt.

Church became another place where he performed. Another place where he felt like he had to clean himself up to be accepted.

He smiled, served, showed up—and slowly bled on the inside.

When Micah finally reached out for help, it didn't come with grace. It came with correction. With subtle withdrawal. With spiritual diagnosis: "Are you sure you're praying enough?" With platitudes: "God won't give you more than you can handle."

With invisible rules: *Don't let your mess be seen too long. Don't stay in the valley too long. Don't question too loudly.*

He didn't need perfect people. He just needed honest ones.

But what he got was distance. What he felt was shame. What he heard was, "Come back when you're better."

No one said it out loud. But silence has a voice of its own.

Micah sat in small groups and listened to people talk about sin like it was always someone else's. He listened to sermons that spoke more about behavior than brokenness. He watched people worship with hands raised while secretly wondering if God really saw the ones who couldn't lift their heads.

And so, he left. Not because he wanted to rebel. But because he was drowning—and the lifeboat was leaking.

It felt like betrayal. He had given so much—his time, his heart, his vulnerability. But when he needed the church to be the hands and feet of Jesus... it became a mirror reflecting his failures.

Micah went through a long, lonely season. Not just of church-lessness—but of spiritual confusion. How could the place that preached love hurt so deeply? How could people who spoke about grace use it like a weapon? How could those who claimed to speak for God miss His heart so badly?

He stopped praying for a while—not because he didn't believe in God, but because he didn't know who he was talking to anymore.

He wasn't angry. He was devastated. He still loved Jesus—but he didn't know how to trust His people.

That's the thing about church hurt. It cuts in a way nothing else does. Because it doesn't come from enemies. It comes from those who say they're family.

But healing came. Slowly. Unpredictably. Through strange places and unexpected people.

Through friends who didn't flinch when he spoke honestly. Through music that reminded him God still heard. Through quiet prayers whispered on long walks, when the walls of a building felt too loud.

Eventually, Micah found a new kind of church. Not a perfect one. Not a flashy one. But one that listened. One that didn't panic at his pain. One that let him sit in the back without asking him to perform. One where people hugged instead of quoted.

It took time to trust again. To believe that God wasn't disappointed in his doubt. That healing didn't require hiding. That the real church—the one Jesus imagined—still existed.

He learned to separate God from people who misrepresented Him. He stopped confusing performance with holiness. He stopped apologizing for his wounds.

Micah forgave the church that broke him. Not because they asked. Not because they changed. But because he refused to carry their weight any longer.

And that forgiveness didn't come wrapped in denial. It came through honesty. Through naming the harm. Through letting go of what they were supposed to be, so he could finally grieve what they weren't.

He found God again. Or maybe—he found Him for the first time, unfiltered. Not through a pulpit. Not through fog machines and lights. But in the quiet places. The broken places. The places the church had told him were too messy to be holy.

Now, when people tell Micah they're done with church, he doesn't preach. He doesn't say, "Well, not all churches..." He doesn't defend the system.

He says, **"Me too."**

And then, **"You're not crazy. And you're not alone."**

Because faith should never come with strings. Because Jesus never demanded performance—He offered presence.

And the church? It's still capable of being beautiful. But only when it remembers who it's meant to reflect.

Micah believes again. But he believes differently now. Wider. Softer. Stronger.

He doesn't go to church to earn grace. He brings grace with him when he walks through the doors. He knows now: the church isn't a building or a brand or a trend.

The Church is the quiet hand on the shoulder. The whispered prayer from a stranger. The honest story that breaks the silence. The table with room for every kind of soul.

It's not where you dress up your wounds. It's where you bring them.

So to the church that broke him—Micah says thank you. Not because it was okay. But because it forced him to find a faith that couldn't be shaken by people.

And to the one who's still carrying church hurt—Micah leans in. Not to explain it away. But to say:

You're not the only one.

You're still loved.

You still belong.

And healing is still possible.

"Surely your goodness and unfailing love will pursue me all the days of my life."

Psalm 23:6 (NIV)

Chapter 24:

To the Moment Grace Found Me

Dear Me (The Broken One),

You were drowning, and no one saw it. Not really. Not in the way you needed them to. You smiled when you were supposed to. You kept going when it hurt. You learned to wear your pain like a second skin, quiet and heavy.

And when it got too loud, too dark—you told yourself it would be easier if you disappeared.

But grace had other plans.

It found you in the silence—not with a spotlight, but with a whisper. Not with answers, but with presence.

It didn't wait for you to be ready. It didn't ask for you to deserve it. It simply came.

You didn't think you were worth saving. But grace never asked for proof. It just said, "Stay."

And somehow, you did.

You stayed. You broke. And then—you began to heal.

This wasn't the end. It was the beginning of everything.

—Micah

Micah had been unraveling for years.

It didn't start all at once. It started slowly—quietly. A slow fade of joy. A gradual dulling of light. A numbness that settled into his bones so gently, he barely noticed it until one day, he woke up and realized he hadn't felt *anything* in a long time.

He kept showing up, though.

To work. To relationships. To responsibilities. He played the role of the functioning man—strong, responsible, reliable. No one knew that beneath the surface, something was splintering.

He didn't even fully know it himself.

The pain didn't come in waves. It came in whispers. Thoughts that tiptoed through his mind at night and pressed into his chest during the day.

You're failing everyone. You're not enough. No one really knows you. If you disappeared, nothing would change.

He thought he could outrun it. Stay busy enough, perform well enough, serve others hard enough. But no matter how far he ran, it always caught up with him—especially when he was alone.

Micah would lie in bed, staring at the ceiling, feeling the weight of everything he couldn't say out loud. His body was present. His spirit was slipping.

He stopped praying. He stopped dreaming. He stopped hoping.

He didn't want to die. He just didn't want to *hurt anymore*.

He remembered one night in particular. The night everything broke.

The house was quiet. Everyone was asleep. But Micah was wide awake, sitting on the edge of his bed, trembling in a darkness that felt thicker than the room itself.

The pressure in his chest felt unbearable. His thoughts spiraled into a place that scared him. It wasn't the first time the thought crossed his mind. But it was the first time it *lingered*.

Maybe everyone would be better off. Maybe the weight he carried would finally lift—if he wasn't here to carry it.

He didn't cry at first. He just sat there, numb. Staring into the quiet. Waiting for it to end.

But then—*he shattered.*

The tears came without permission. His body folded in on itself. His breath hitched. His hands shook. The dam he had built to hold back years of grief, guilt, fear, and shame—finally broke.

And then, in the middle of that storm… came stillness.

Not in his body. Not in his mind. But somewhere deeper.

A whisper. Not his own.

"You're not alone. And this is not the end."

He couldn't explain it. Couldn't prove it. But he felt it—*presence.*

Holy. Quiet. Gentle. Like someone was sitting beside him, even though the room was still empty.

It wasn't a rescue. It was a *reminder.*

A flicker of something he hadn't felt in years: *grace.*

Micah collapsed into that moment. Not because everything was fixed—but because something inside of him had shifted.

He whispered the words he hadn't said in so long: "God… if You're still there… I need You."

No fireworks followed. No miracles. But there was breath. And for the first time in weeks, he let it fill his lungs.

That night became a turning point—not because it erased the darkness, but because it *interrupted* it.

Micah began to slowly open the locked doors of his heart. First to God. Then to people. Then to himself.

He told a friend what had happened. Then another. He made a call to a counselor. Booked an appointment. Showed up—terrified, but honest.

And grace met him again. In the office chair. In the silence between words. In the tears he finally gave himself permission to cry.

It wasn't about solving everything. It was about *naming it*.

The shame. The exhaustion. The fear. The lie that he had to do it all alone.

Micah learned something life-changing: Healing doesn't happen *instead of* pain. It happens *through* it.

He started going to therapy regularly. He started opening up at church. He picked up his Bible again—hesitant, but willing. He didn't find a checklist for healing. He found a God who wept. A Savior who sat in gardens sweating blood. A Shepherd who left the ninety-nine for the one drowning in his own mind.

That kind of grace didn't judge him. It *sat with him*.

And over time, grace didn't just carry him—it began to *reshape* him.

Micah forgave himself. He looked back on his younger self—not with shame, but with *compassion*.

He began to see his scars not as evidence of failure, but of survival. Proof that he had been to the edge—and chose to stay.

He reconnected with his kids in deeper ways. He shared his story. Quietly at first. Then more boldly. And he found that vulnerability wasn't weakness. It was *invitation*.

People leaned in when he stopped pretending.

Micah learned that trust doesn't require perfection—just presence. So he kept showing up. To his kids. To his wife. To himself.

Not as a hero. Not as someone with all the answers. But as someone who knew the darkness—and still chose the light.

He still had days. Hard ones. But now, he had tools. Now, he had truth. Now, he had *people*.

And more than that—he had *grace*.

Not the kind you sing about once a week. The kind that *pulls you from the floor when you don't want to get up*.

The kind that doesn't shame you when you're broken—it *holds* you there.

The kind that says, *"You're not too far gone. You're not too broken. You're not disqualified."*

Micah's life didn't become perfect. But it became real.

Full of honest conversations. Soft prayers whispered in dark rooms. Laughter that no longer felt borrowed. Tears that didn't scare him anymore.

He became a man not healed *despite* the pain, but because he *faced* it.

And in that pain, he found God. Not in the explanation. But in the *presence*.

The God who didn't fix everything right away. But stayed.

Micah had spent so many years running—from pain, from shame, from truth.

But now?

Now, he was standing.

Maybe a little shaky. Maybe still healing. But *standing, nonetheless.*

Because grace had found him—right in the mess—and whispered," This is not the end. This is where it begins."

And that?

That changed everything.

*"And I will give you a new heart,
and a new spirit I will put within you"*

Ezekiel 36.26 (NIV)

Chapter 25:

To the Me Who Finally Believed It

Dear Me (The One Who Finally Believed It),

You stopped waiting for someone else to say it first. Stopped looking for permission to matter. Stopped measuring your value by what you could offer or how well you could hide the hurt.

You believed it.

Not just with your mouth. With your heart. With your breath. With the way you woke up and chose to stay.

You believed you were more than your worst days. More than the names you were called. More than the stories you used to tell yourself in the dark.

You believed you were worthy. Even before the healing was finished. Even when the cracks were still showing.

And maybe that's what changed everything. Not perfection. Not closure. But belief.

You finally believed you were loved. And that changed everything.

—Micah

There wasn't one moment. Not a spotlight epiphany or a big speech in front of a mirror. It came slowly. Quietly. Like light sneaking through blinds after a long night.

Micah didn't notice it at first. He just started living differently. Started breathing a little easier. Started looking people in the eye instead of the floor.

There was no parade. No medal. Just peace. Just *finally feeling like he belonged in his own story.*

He had spent most of his life trying to earn his place. Through achievements. Through kindness. Through silence. Through faith. If he could be good enough, maybe he'd be worth something.

But healing didn't come in being good. It came in being honest.

And when Micah finally stopped running from himself—when he stopped performing and started *being*—he discovered a truth that stayed:

He was already enough.

Not in a feel-good, self-help way. In a deep, steady, soul-settling way. The kind that doesn't need approval to stand on.

Micah began to laugh without guilt. Rest without shame. Say "no" without apology. Say "yes" to things that didn't have outcomes attached.

He forgave himself. Not just the surface-level forgiveness. But the kind that said: "I see what you did. I know why. And I still choose grace."

He stopped needing to be rescued. And started recognizing that he had learned to rescue himself—not from pain, but from the lie that he wasn't worth the effort.

Micah stopped calling himself broken. Not because the wounds weren't real. But because healing had rewired his understanding of what it meant to be whole.

He was whole now. Cracks and all.

He didn't feel the need to explain his story anymore. Not to justify it. Not to defend it. Just to live it.

Because this—this quiet confidence, this gentle steadiness—was the fruit of every hard conversation, every lonely night, every tear shed in the dark.

And when people asked, "How did you get here?" He didn't say it was easy. He didn't pretend it was fast. He just smiled and said, "I stayed."

He stayed through the silence. Stayed through the relapse. Stayed through the grief and guilt and hard grace.

And in the staying, he became.

Micah began to notice things he used to miss. Sunrises. His wife's quiet presence. The sound of his children's laughter echoing off the walls.

He didn't feel like an intruder in his own life anymore. He belonged here. And for the first time, he didn't doubt it.

He wasn't trying to prove anything. He was just living. Loving. Being.

And that was more than enough.

Now, when he meets people who remind him of who he used to be—when he sees the haunted eyes, the held breath, the quiet despair—he doesn't pity them. He sees them. He remembers. And he leans in.

"You're not too far gone," he says. Not as a cliché. But as someone who once believed he was. And then lived long enough to know better.

Micah doesn't call himself "in recovery" anymore. Not because the work is done. But because the shame is.

He doesn't flinch at his past. He honors it. Because it brought him here.

And here? Here is good.

Not perfect. But rooted. Clear-eyed. Soft-hearted. At peace.

Micah finally believed it.

And that—more than any turning point or redemption arc—was the miracle.

"I am confident of this very thing, that He who began a good work in you will carry it on to completion"

Philippians 1:6 (NIV)

Epilogue:

To You

Dear You (Still Becoming),

This wasn't just my story. It was ours.

If you saw yourself in these pages—if something stirred, something ached, something broke open or quietly began—I need you to know: That wasn't an accident.

You matter. Your story matters. Even the chapters you've tried to tear out. Even the pages stained with silence. Even the lines still unfinished.

You don't have to be whole to be worthy. You don't have to be healed to be held. You don't have to have it all figured out to be fully, deeply loved exactly as you are.

The road is messy. The climb is hard. But grace walks with you every step of the way. Not behind you with judgment. Not ahead of you with impossible standards. But with you—here, now.

You are not beyond redemption. You are not too far gone. You are not the worst thing you've done or the worst thing that's been done to you. You are not a mistake. You are not disqualified.

You are becoming. And that becoming—that stumbling, rising, wrestling, reaching—is holy work.

Keep breathing. Keep hoping. Keep showing up for your own life. Keep writing your story, one honest, brave sentence at a time.

The stars don't shine despite the dark. They shine because of it.

And you, friend—you are one of them.

I see you. I believe in you. I'm walking with you.

—Micah

Micah remembered a night long before healing had a name.

He was sitting alone in the back corner of a quiet coffee shop. The lights were warm, but they didn't touch the places inside him that had gone cold. His journal sat beside him, untouched. The pen looked like a dare.

Around him, people laughed and sipped coffee and planned their tomorrows like they expected to wake up happy.

Micah watched them like someone looking through glass—on the outside, breathing the same air, but disconnected from whatever it was that made life feel full.

He wondered what it must be like to feel light. To not carry everything all the time. To not constantly wonder if you were too broken to be loved.

That night, he didn't write.

He went home. Stood in front of the mirror. And saw every invisible crack.

Adoption. Abandonment. Bullying. Shame. Failure. Fear.

He saw a man barely holding it together. And for the first time, he didn't look away.

Because somewhere, buried beneath the ache, was something else—something small, something flickering.

A whisper of hope. A defiant little ember that refused to go out.

That was the beginning.

Not of healing, not yet. But of something more important: honesty. That quiet, tired, almost-broken moment was the true beginning. Because it was the moment he stopped performing. Stopped hiding. Stopped trying to be someone enough to be loved—and started becoming someone who already was.

Micah would go on to write letters. To the versions of himself he once feared. The ones he resented. The ones he tried to forget.

To the boy who was chosen—but didn't feel wanted. To the quiet kid left out of every lunch table. To the soldier who wore a uniform like armor to outrun shame. To the husband who failed. To the father who doubted he was enough. To the man who wanted to die—but stayed anyway.

Each letter peeled something open. Not just memory. But meaning. Each one pulled truth out of places Micah had buried it for safety.

And now, he was writing to you.

Because stories are meant to be shared. Because healing was never meant to stay locked in a journal.

Micah thought he was writing to his past. But in the end, he was writing to your present.

To the quiet battles you're still fighting. To the words you haven't yet said. To the breath you're holding, hoping someone sees you.

If you've ever sat in a room full of people and felt like you didn't belong—if you've ever wondered whether you were too much or not enough—if you've ever stood in front of a mirror and felt more fracture than flesh—you are the reason this book was written.

Because Micah didn't survive just to say he made it. He survived to say you can too.

Not perfectly. Not painlessly. But honestly. And honestly? That's more than enough.

Grace doesn't need you to get it all right. Faith doesn't need you to fake it. Healing doesn't need you to rush.

Healing starts the moment you stop pretending. When you stop performing. When you finally say, "I'm tired," and let yourself be seen.

And the miracle? It's not that Micah found his way. It's that when he stopped running, He found God already there—in the mess.

Not the cleaned-up version. Not the polished, performative version. The God who stays. Who sits on the bathroom floor with you. Who whispers, "You're not alone."

Micah found people who didn't run. He found love that didn't flinch. He found breath when he thought he had none left.

And if he could find those things—so can you.

Micah used to believe his story ended in pain.

Now he knows—pain was just the place where the light came in.

He used to think he had to be someone else to be worthy. Now he knows he was worthy all along.

He used to think healing meant fixing every broken piece. Now he knows healing is learning to live gently with the cracks.

Wherever you are on your journey—whether you're deep in the mess, climbing out, or standing on the edge of hope—you are not behind. You are not too broken. You are not too late.

You're becoming. And becoming is brave.

There will still be hard days. You might still feel like running. You might fall back into old patterns or wrestle with old lies.

But don't mistake struggle for failure. And don't mistake feeling lost for being lost.

You're here. Reading this.

Breathing.

Beating.

Becoming.

Micah closes his journal, the final page now filled. Not with answers. But with peace. Not with a neat ending. But with an honest one.

He walks outside. The sky is dark—quiet, soft, waiting.

And then he looks up.

Stars.

Scattered across the night like reminders.

They don't shine despite the darkness. They shine because of it. Just like him. Just like you.

He breathes in deep. Let's it fill him, steady him.

And whispers one final word:

Thank You.

For the pain.

For the grace.

For the becoming.

For the story that's only just beginning.

"The journey isn't finished, and neither are you.
Becoming takes time – and that's holy work"

—*Unknown*

To the Letters Still Unwritten

Dear Me (Still Becoming),

You've come so far.

This book—these letters—they were never the whole story. They were the truth as you could tell it then. But healing isn't a final destination. It's a rhythm. A return. A choice we keep making even when our voice shakes.

There are still letters I haven't written.

Because I'm still becoming.

There are still pieces I don't know how to put into words. Still wounds that ache on quiet nights. Still questions I'm learning to live with. Not everything has been tied up neatly. Not every pain has found its purpose.

And that's okay.

This final chapter isn't a conclusion. It's an invitation. An acknowledgment that even after healing… we're still human.

So here are some letters I haven't finished yet—some because they're too tender, some because they're still unfolding, and some because I haven't found the courage to fully face them.

But they matter.

Because I'm still healing.

And maybe, you are too.

So here they are:

To the Father I Never Knew

I've imagined your face a thousand times. I've blamed you, missed you, resented you, and longed for your approval all in the same breath. I don't know your story. But I carry the absence of it like a shadow. And some days… I still wonder if you ever wondered about me.

To the Child I Might Have Been

I'm sorry I silenced you.

You were loud with wonder, full of questions, messy and magical. But I tried to grow up too fast, thinking maturity meant muting you.

I miss your courage. I miss your curiosity. I'm trying to let you speak again.

To the Apology I Still Owe

There are people I've hurt. People I dismissed. People I didn't love well.

And while some bridges have burned, the ashes still whisper. I don't expect reconciliation. But I pray they've found peace.

And I pray I learn to do better with the time I have left.

To the Body I Struggled to Accept

I judged you. I punished you. I tried to shrink you into someone else's standard.

But you've carried me through every storm. You've held me through sickness, joy, and every quiet morning. You didn't deserve the war I waged against you. You deserve rest. You deserve love.

And I'm learning to give it to you.

To the Faith I'm Still Rebuilding

We had a break. A brutal one. I questioned everything. I still do sometimes. But even in the doubt, I feel something sacred—like grace has been waiting in the hallway the whole time. I'm not where I was. I'm not where I thought I'd be. But maybe that's where faith really lives—in the tension.

To the Anger I Was Taught to Hide

You weren't wrong. You were honest. But I buried you because I thought emotions like you made me weak. Now I know better. You're not the enemy—you're a signal. And I'm learning to listen without letting you lead.

To the Silence That Shaped Me

You taught me to observe, to wait, to watch.
But also… to fear speaking.
To second-guess my worth.
To settle for being unseen.
I'm finding my voice now—not to be loud, but to be whole.

To the Friend I Let Go

I miss you.
Not every day. Not in every way. But sometimes, in the soft quiet, I remember what we had.
I don't know if I handled it right. I hope you're well.
And I hope you know… I loved you, even in the letting go.

To the Future I'm Still Afraid Of

I've made plans. I've dreamed big. I've imagined better. But some nights, fear still whispers that I'll mess it all up. That I'll slip, fall, lose it all. But I'm learning not to let fear do the dreaming for me anymore.

The future doesn't have to be figured out—it just has to be faced.

To the Man I'm Still Becoming

I see you. You're not perfect. You still stumble. You still wrestle. But you've stopped hiding. You're showing up. You're speaking truth. You're choosing healing again and again.
And that? That's more than enough.

Closing Words

These are the letters I haven't finished. The ones I'm still living. Some I may never write. Some may only ever exist as a whisper between me and God.
But that's the beauty of becoming.
We're not finished.
We're not failures because we're still healing.
We're just… human.
And that, my friend, is holy ground.

—Micah

Author Bio:

Matt is a veteran, husband, father of four, and storyteller with a passion for helping others find healing through honesty, faith, and redemption. After years of wrestling with identity, self-worth, and depression, Matt discovered the power of grace—and now writes to reach others walking through similar battles.

In *Dear Me, I Found You*, his debut book, Matt channels his own journey into the voice of Micah, a character shaped by real struggles and hard-won hope. When he's not writing, you can find him running a coffee shop, raising his kids, and reminding people that they're never too far gone to be found.